THE BOOK OF HOMES

Other Books by Andrea Bajani Available in English Translation

Every Promise

If You Kept a Record of Sins

Praise for *If You Kept a Record of Sins* by Andrea Bajani (translated by Elizabeth Harris)

"Writing such as this makes me happy again, and it gives me comfort, because it is itself a form of resistance." —**Antonio Tabucchi**

"[Bajani's] calm, elegant prose stands on its own, defying commentary. Bajani understands how the wounded often remain wounded, cut off from others and themselves. Such is the tragedy of the human story, which is somehow made less tragic by his remarkable ability to illuminate it for us."

—**Elaine Margolin**, *Los Angeles Review of Books*

"Andrea Bajani's haunting portrait of a mother-son relationship accumulates with the quiet urgency of a snowstorm. The impact is shattering, pure. With themes of distance and dislocation at its heart, this celebrated novel by one of Italy's most talented young writers now resonates in English thanks to Elizabeth Harris's limpid translation." —**Jhumpa Lahiri**

"*If You Kept a Record of Sins* is written with grace and calm control. It deals with loss, especially the loss of a mother, with a chiseled sense of truth. Each image and each moment are captured with exquisite emotional accuracy. The connection between the past and the present is dramatized with skill. The protagonist is, like the author himself, someone on whom nothing is lost."

—**Colm Tóibín**

"Part of a brilliant new generation of Italian writers that includes names like Paolo Giordano, Elena Ferrante, and Mirko Sabatino."

—**Fernando Hernández Urías**, *Chilango*

"Without a doubt, one of the most powerful voices from the generation of authors born in the 1970s."

—**Guadalupe Nettel**, *Revista UNAM*

"The magic of this story lies entirely in the telling—in the delicate balancing of select, sharply depicted images within a spare, measured narrative that simmers with barely restrained emotional tension . . . Reading fiction this well-crafted is a joy."

—**Joseph Schreiber**, *Rough Ghosts*

The Book of Homes

Andrea Bajani

Translated from the Italian by Elizabeth Harris

DEEP VELLUM PUBLISHING

DALLAS, TEXAS

Deep Vellum Publishing
3000 Commerce St., Dallas, Texas 75226
deepvellum.org · @deepvellum

Deep Vellum is a 501c3 nonprofit literary arts organization founded in 2013 with the mission to bring the world into conversation through literature.

Originally published in Italian as *Il libro delle case* in 2021 by Giangiacomo Feltrinelli Editore, Milan, Italy.
Published by arrangement with The Italian Literary Agency

Support for this publication has been provided in part by grants from the National Endowment for the Arts, the Texas Commission on the Arts, the City of Dallas Office of Arts and Culture, the Communities Foundation of Texas, and the Addy Foundation.

This work was translated with the support of the Centro per il libro e la lettura del Ministero della Cultura italiano (Center for Books and Reading of the Italian Ministry of Culture).

LIBRARY OF CONGRESS CATALOGING-IN-PUBLICATION DATA
Names: Bajani, Andrea, 1975- author. | Harris, Elizabeth, 1963- translator.

Title: The book of homes / Andrea Bajani ; translated from the Italian by Elizabeth Harris.
Other titles: Libro delle case. English
Description: First English edition. | Dallas, Texas : Deep Vellum Publishing, 2025.
Identifiers: LCCN 2025007871 (print) | LCCN 2025007872 (ebook) | ISBN 9781646053810 (trade paperback) | ISBN 9781646053933 (ebook)
Subjects: LCGFT: Novels.
Classification: LCC PQ4862.A35245 L5313 2025 (print) | LCC PQ4862.A35245 (ebook) | DDC 853/.914--dc23/eng/20250303
LC record available at https://lccn.loc.gov/2025007871
LC ebook record available at https://lccn.loc.gov/2025007872

Cover art and design by Jeremy Hughes
Interior layout and typesetting by KGT

PRINTED IN THE UNITED STATES OF AMERICA

Xavier replied that a home is not a linen closet or a bird in a cage but the presence of the person we love. And then he told her that he himself had no home, or rather, to put it another way, that his home was in his pace, in his walk, in his journeys. That his home was wherever new horizons opened. That he could only live by going from one dream to another, from one landscape to another . . .

Milan Kundera, *Life Is Elsewhere*
(translated by Aaron Asher)

1

Underground Home, 1976

His first home has three bedrooms, a living room, kitchen, and bathroom. The baby's bedroom—and this baby we'll refer to as "I"—is actually a closet with a cot crammed inside. A bit damp, like the rest of the apartment. There are no windows, but the room is comfortable and close to the kitchen. And the clattering of dishes, the tick-ticking of the knife on the cutting board, the water running from the faucet are probably I's first memories, even if he doesn't remember them. Just as he doesn't remember the soft thud of the refrigerator door closing, or the resistant tearing as it opens. A small polyphony in the kitchen: metal percussions, counterpoints of clanging ceramic and running water and the hum of the refrigerator and the hood fan.

His home is below ground level. The apartment can only be reached by a spiral staircase or else the elevator. The lobby, a strip of red carpet leading to these stairs, smells much different than the floor below, with its dampness and basement smell. And really, this is the same level as the basement, this apartment where I's family lives, and there are two other massive wooden doors, and beyond them, other undetermined families.

—

But the Underground Home isn't entirely below ground level. The dining room, kitchen, bathroom, and two bedrooms face two internal courtyards. Dining room, kitchen, and bath on one side, two bedrooms on the other. The internal courtyards, or cement yards, are enclosed by a series of condominiums, five to six stories high, built in the 1950s and 1960s.

Stepping out into the courtyard, you're forced to tilt back your head. I's grandma—from now on, "Grandma"—has the same routine every morning: she steps out, tilts back her head, and looks up at the sky to check the weather. Then she goes back in.

From inside the Underground Home, it always seems cloudy. The windows facing the two cement yards don't bring in enough daylight. That's why you have to turn on a lamp in the hall when you come in; the lights stay on at all times.

In that darkness, I begins to crawl. The objects and furniture push their shadows over the floor, spilling everywhere, flooding the apartment, climbing onto side tables, windowsills, the ceramic fruit basket that stays at the center of the dining room table. I learns how to move around among those shadows, to trample them, be overwhelmed by them. Sometimes, crawling and disappearing inside a shadow, or just sticking out a hand or foot, abandoning them to the glowing light: I goes to pieces in the darkness, streaks of him left on the rug.

In the Underground Home, the lights go off only when it's time for bed or time to leave: the apartment is consigned to darkness, its natural element. Four turns of the key, loud voices on the stairs, then silence. And the shadows slip off the objects entirely, dive onto the floor, subdue every square centimeter, capture the place.

—

The courtyard facing the kitchen, bathroom, and dining room is where Turtle lives. Lives more or less hidden behind flowerpots or inside her carapace. It's rare to see her step out from cover. Only when Grandma comes does she run to meet her, scuffling across the courtyard, shell repeatedly hitting the ground, a rhythm identical to her joy. Grandma picks her up, talks to her; Turtle waves her four wrinkly legs, testing out this assisted flight among those buildings that force the sky into a square where she might be free. Then she returns to her place behind the pots, dragging the lettuce leaf that Grandma has brought her and that she'll greedily, stingily devour, shredding the leaf with her hard beak, until it disappears.

Turtle is the first animal I has met in the Underground Home. Then again, I is the only human—aside from Grandma—that Turtle has ever let see her head, as it slides out from her shell.

I looks for her in the courtyard, knows where to find her: he crawls until he's close, scrambling across the cement yard, every day, his rhythmic knees, faster. The two always meet behind the flower-pots. I slaps his palms on Turtle's carapace, an excited, merry drum-ming. That tribal drumming—I sitting on the ground, on the soft throne of his own diaper—is probably I's first accomplished ritual. I beats time on her armor and Turtle stretches out her neck.

Turtle is also the first being whose example I follows: unlike most other children who detest every kind of vegetable, I demands lettuce. Even his movements are turtle-induced: long periods of stillness, in various hiding places, then accelerating sharply down the hall.

When the two find themselves face to face on the ground, I squeals with laughter. Then he puts his small, bare foot in Turtle's face, and with his big toe, rubs her head. Because I's big toe and Turtle's head are the same shape, I is certain his head is his foot. So in his vision of his first two years of life, I is a turtle with two heads. Turtle and I greet each other through the child's feet.

The Underground Home is on one of the seven hills of the city of Rome.

Every day, at the top of the hill, two soldiers of the Italian army roll a cannon out to the ramparts. At the stroke of noon, the cannon fires on Rome. The crowd claps at this staged scene, the Italian army shooting—blanks—at their capital. The children often cry at the blast, while the parents vainly attempt to explain the meaning of this fiction, the difference here from reality. The explosion can be heard for kilometers, its shock waves carrying over the landscape, this same landscape that those present shoot with their cameras.

In the Underground Home there's Father, Mother, Sister, Grandma. And I.

2

Home of the Radiator, 1998

IT WAS GROUNDBREAKING, BUYING THIS television now sitting on the fake terracotta-tile floor. A small set—fourteen inches, according to the box—with the power to draw people to the ground: as soon as it's plugged in, I lies on the floor on his side, like an Etruscan on his tomb, and stares at the bright screen.

Bought out of pure instinct, millions of years of evolution for the species, acquired knowledge and genes. Still unfamiliar with Turin, he went to the one electronics store he knew of, that he'd seen from the tram every day for ten months: outside the city, by the bypass entrance, selling TVs, blenders, washing machines, many other appliances, arranged in the shop window, a landscape of efficiency.

And so the bus trip to his first home after graduating from college was a ritual of lifting. I got on the 55 with the large Panasonic box, apologizing as he went, blaming the carton. He set the box on the first free seat and stood guard beside it. At the twelfth stop, counted through door puffs, he got off, walked three hundred meters carrying this box, then up four flights of stairs.

Watching him: his roommate (the owner of the apartment, a

13

man of about sixty, showing signs of personal wreckage), secretly jubilant and outwardly disapproving: not wanting to pay the state fee, not wanting the hassle, but knowing he'd benefit. Standing at the door, watching I pull the TV from the Styrofoam, place it on the floor, plug it in, and push the power button. On the first viable channel, a female newscaster, well-dressed, the first female presence ever in the room.

That this home is temporary is obvious from the lack of a wardrobe in I's room, though it's been a month and a half since he first stepped through the door. His open suitcase by the cot serves as a dresser. Plus, there's no real agreement, nothing signed between him and his roommate. Money exchanges hands at the end of the month and the only other condition is that on Tuesday afternoons, I has to be out until dinner, to allow his roommate his weekly sodomy.

As for I's sexual activity—the unspoken part of this agreement —he has the entire weekend, when his roommate disappears, leaves the city.

I won't be there long; this is clear to them both, just as it's clear to them both that the memory of it, this living together, will be better than living this every day. The truth is, they have little interaction at all save for dividing the shelves in the refrigerator and then a common courtesy sanitized by discretion. The life going on here is mainly a bedroom life. The rest of the apartment doesn't exist: the kitchen is blind (with a grille facing the stairs) and has hardly the space to maneuver, and a table for one. And the entryway is almost entirely taken up by a kerosene radiator, the only source of heat. The bathroom right beside it is the warmest room in the place.

The radiator is the reason why life in the bedrooms is a life of open doors. The alternative is privacy at outdoor temperatures; but it's January and outside the first snow is falling, that empty promise first of Christmas, then New Year's. The Turin rooftops are white, and so is the train station, two blocks away, the snow softening the whistling of the trains as they come and go. So privacy is two sweaters and chattering teeth.

It's why I has cut off the fingertips to his gloves. Within that icy room, he warms his fingers by striking the keyboard of an old computer, rescued in extremis from the dumpster where a friend was planning to chuck it. An extinct species, discontinued, the monitor screen arthritic, exhausted, with barely visible images, and very slow. But it's the first computer I has ever owned, and there's no amount of cold that will reduce the impact of what I calls *The Revolution*, the coup that over the course of a few weeks has supplanted the television set, pilloried on the floor, condemned to die.

So what the windows see on the other side of the street, every evening, into the night, is a boy buried in sweaters, a cap sometimes pulled down over his ears, typing away on a keyboard, on a desk that's a piece of particleboard propped on two trestles and clearly too high for the boy's chair. And all of this blurring in the falling snow, at a distance, if someone's actually watching.

What's impossible to see, no doubt, is the gap between I's outburst of typing and the technology limping up behind; between the pounding rush of words and the screen standing white, stunned and weary, then finally spitting those words back all at once, on delay, when I's already left the sentence, his hands motionless, in thoughtful pause. Fingers raised over the keys, he sees the words stepping out from that whiteness, a column of them, proceeding all in a row, then rushing forward, only stopping if a period commands it. Afterwards, I reads—stunned himself now, and moved—what all these words, standing at attention, have come to tell him in the cold.

3

Family's Home, 2009

THE FAMILY'S HOME CONSISTS OF three rooms plus a kitchen. The entry hall is dimly lit. A small table to the right of the door is where they automatically toss their keys. A floor of yellow and gray granolithic tiles, ill-conceived, extends into the kitchen.

The two rooms off this entry hall, the eat-in living room and Wife and I's bedroom, both with wood floors. The eat-in living room has a simple sofa bed, sand-colored upholstery. Such an ordinary, plain couch that once seen, it's forgotten, like it's not there at all. In front of this couch, the TV. Not much more to say about this room: a table, cherry finish, that can seat six, four chairs carefully positioned on opposite sides.

At the back of the room, a window with a view of a rooftop terrace across the street, where an old couple has lunch and dinner in the summer and then in the winter, becomes a storage area. Beyond that terrace, the Alps. As it begins to warm up, I will open the window and spend a lot of time there, elbows on the sill. Now and then Little Girl's head pokes up as well. Sometimes just for a second, other times she stops beside him. The moment someone shows up on that terrace, Little Girl silently waves hello; another hand, mute, good-natured, waves back. A long-held custom that hasn't turned into a relationship, has never blossomed into a verbal greeting, and has never lost its gentleness. A matter left entirely to hands.

All around the Home, early twentieth-century buildings, nice middle-class people wandering around, pastry shops, Sunday pastries, restaurants full of nicely—tastefully—dressed families. Two hundred meters away, Turin's main railway station.

Wife and I's bedroom is the largest in the apartment—roughly thirty square meters—and split into a night zone and day zone. A queen-size bed with a light wood frame stands at the back of the room by a glass door onto a balcony. On either side of the bed are two wooden cubes, much like fruit crates, but designed for the wealthy, post-agricultural clientele that shop at the supermarket. You can tell I's side by the precarious tower of books. More books lie spine up, flipped open, on the floor, like dragonflies, waiting. Other dragonflies are scattered throughout the apartment, on the armrests of the couch, the kitchen table.

The so-called day zone of the bedroom is, essentially, Wife's writing desk: with highlighter pens, a basket containing scissors and staples, notebooks, a laptop and printer. On the writing surface, pink and yellow Post-its.

The last room is Little Girl's.

The frosted-glass door is always closed. Through this glass, even coming closer, you wouldn't see much: it's mostly covered by a sheet of paper taped at the corners. A poster that Little Girl can see from her bed, the back of it facing those on the outside. Hers is a room thought of only as an inside: outside is an inside-out inside, the seam-side world.

When she goes to school, the room's left open. Wife goes in and cleans; normally I won't go past the doorway, but it's hard not to look in. The floor, the usual yellow and gray tiles. Bed against one wall. Facing him, a white, two-doored wardrobe coated in a moss of stickers, and a couple of photos. One with Girlfriends, another with Little Girl's Father. Beside the wardrobe, on a shelf, a stack of schoolbooks and a photo of her and I hugging, taken by Wife. All told, no longer a nursery: a room.

Opposite this room is the kitchen with its few meters of granolithic tiles. On the wall, three sets of cabinets, cherry-colored, upper and lower, clearly fitted into this space. The countertop has been lopped off on one side, the particleboard edge showing. At the center, the stovetop, a convection oven below. Against the wall, a small table and three chairs. Hanging on the wall, a whiteboard with Little Girl's week divided into columns of days and rows of hours.

Outside, a view onto the garages and the apartment railings of other buildings. Then the hills beyond. A kitchen cabinet, due to a lack of space, has been banished to the balcony and is used for storage.

For the most part, you can guess by the furnishings that the Family's Home is actually two sets of furniture stuck together to make a nonexistent third. It's easy to tell whose are whose—those belonging to I, those belonging to Wife + Little Girl—it's easy to reconstruct the two original apartments, these two lives glued together into one new experiment.

That's why I spends a lot of time in the main room, sitting at the table or else on the couch. Especially when he's in a bad mood or they've fought, which doesn't happen often: his old furniture is his embassy, where he beats a retreat. He'll collect himself, on the couch, heels drawn up, feet not touching the floor. He stays there until he feels better, then he'll get up and move around the apartment. Often, though, it's Wife who comes to him to make up, and he opens the embassy door. He moves to one side, lets her sit, welcomes her with his eyes. When she gets up again, their peace made, I sets his feet back down.

The sight of Little Girl, asleep on the couch nearly every afternoon, her math or science book on the cushion, pencil on the floor, is still something that startles him.

4

Underground Home, 1978

ONE OF THE FIRST THINGS I remembers is Father shut up in his room for days, maybe weeks.

It's early spring; in the two cement yards enclosed by buildings, there's finally sun. Not much and not for long. An apparition showing up twice a day. The first time, when the sun is high above, so around 12:40 during this period: a time when sunlight spills over the yards, but little more than a bucketful.

The second time, the sunlight arrives from the east, in the early evening, around 6:30. Only a ray of light slipping between two buildings. But after working its way through, this ray expands, descending, taking hold, lighting a meter and a half of ground. At that point, a regular drumming is heard: Turtle appears, runs out from behind a flowerpot, plastron scraping. She catches that ray on the fly, a tennis player. Then she stops, head out, in its spotlight.

If she's lucky, she'll stay like this as long as the evening sunray lasts. Then it fizzles out and Turtle slowly returns the way she came. If things go badly for her, I comes running—and usually screaming —and turns Turtle into a drum.

—

Father is always shut up in his room: he only leaves for the bathroom and afterwards, he shuts himself back inside.

Often, he doesn't eat, rarely with Sister, Mother, Grandma, and I.

If Father's not there, Grandma's voice is nearly always the one that's heard. During meals, the TV speaks, but if Father's there, this voice is quiet. The TV speaks of a kidnapped politician, shut up in an apartment and condemned to die. There's a photo of the man holding up a newspaper; it's to demonstrate that the man—that day—is still alive.

You can't tell where he is from the photo. There's only a flag behind him.

No one at the table is really watching or listening to the TV. But the TV throws light on them, a sheaf of light within the rectangle of that object, which then floods over the table. The only one outside this light, at times, is I; he runs around the apartment, falls, but doesn't cry. He always stops outside the closed door to Father's room.

Then he races back, and into the dining room, and sees Mother, Grandma, and Sister inside the light of the TV set; and he goes inside as well, just like Turtle in the afternoon sunlight. The TV spills the man with the newspaper over their heads.

The screen is the entrance to a tunnel tying the Underground Home to the apartment where the man's being held. Only I can enter here, and only crawling on all fours.

Sister's already too big.

For Mother and Grandma, this wouldn't be graceful.

But I can easily slip inside that rectangle of light; he'd just have to crawl a little—who knows for how long—and then pop out the other end, near Prisoner and the newspaper.

But the others and I don't really consider this option: they stay where they are, and the TV pours its entire contents over their heads. Plus, since testing out and then adopting his upright position, I's not particularly interested in returning to all fours.

He only does it sometimes with Turtle, but this is a long-established relationship.

When lunch is over, Mother carries a plate into Father's room. I follows behind her, but stays outside; she gestures to him, then shuts the door.

A short while later, Mother comes out again and talks with Grandma as she washes the dishes.

But sometimes Mother also leaves the door ajar, if I's not hot on her heels, and once he poked his head through the crack and saw them both sitting on the couch. Father had his head in his hands; Mother was near him, not talking, not touching him, her knees together.

On the phone, Grandma says her son—Father—is scared.

"He won't leave the apartment because he's afraid they're going to hurt him."

"He hit someone he shouldn't have."

She says you have to be sure of yourself before you pretend to be strong.

The phone is in the kitchen, by a small table and a chair. There's a whiteboard above the table where Grandma can jot down notes so she won't forget.

When Grandma talks about Father on the phone, she pulls the

door closed, but I pushes it open because that's how he gets through to go find Turtle out in the cement yard.

Grandma's words fall on his head as he goes by; they stay in his hair until—with him kicking and screaming a thousand screams—Mother washes them out.

Agenzia del Territorio
CATASTO FABBRICATI
Ufficio Provinciale di

Dichiarazione protocollo n.   del
Planimetria di u.i.u. in Comune di
Via   civ.

Identificativi Catastali: Compilata da:
   Sezione:
   Foglio: Iscritto all'albo:
                                             Geometri
Particella:
Subalterno: Prov.   N.

Scheda n. 1   Scala 1:100

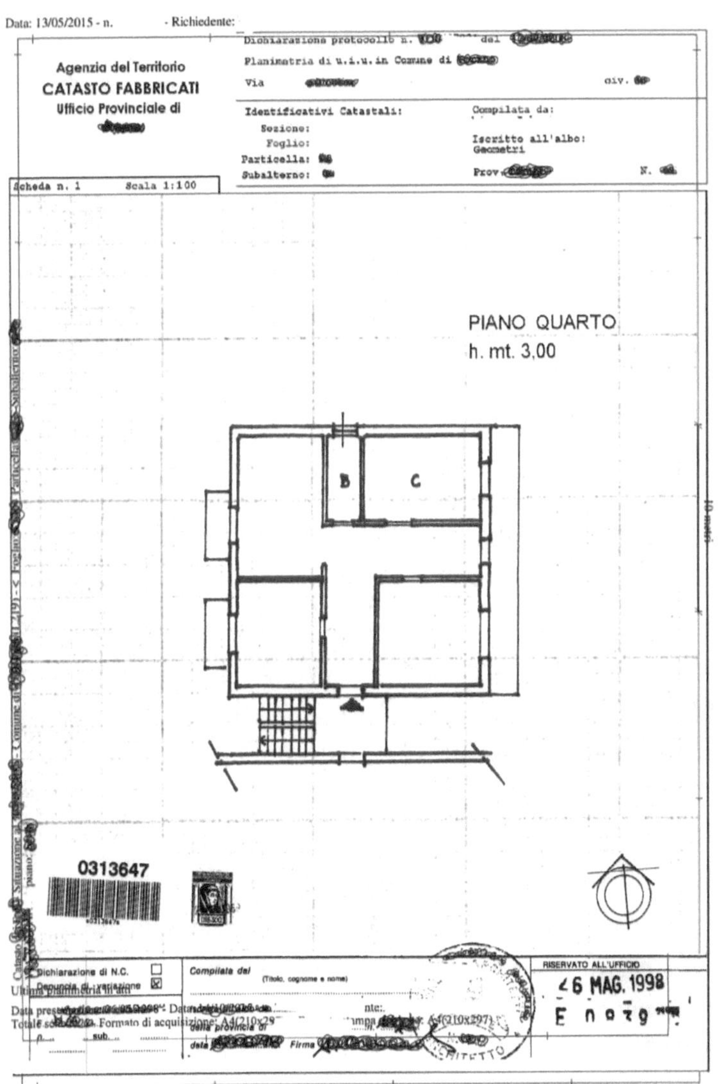

Dichiarazione di N.C.   ☐   Compilata dal
Ultima planimetria in atti ☒   (Titolo, cognome e nome)

Data present   Data   nte:
Totale sc   Formato di acquisizione: A4(210x29   mpa   (210x297)
    n.   sub.   della provincia di
                                           data   Firma

RISERVATO ALL'UFFICIO
26 MAG. 1998

5

Home of Words, 2010

It's less than a kilometer from the Family's Home, past the Turin train station.

Every morning, I leaves the apartment, walks through the station's atrium, and makes his way to the Home of Words.

A seven-minute walk; eight if he stops and looks at the Departures board. Some days he doesn't look up. Other times he does, glancing up at the destinations, imagining himself in some of those places. Then he keeps walking, cutting through the crowd; he comes out here, in this other part of the city.

Before, there was gunfire here, and people stayed inside. Sleeping meant earplugs or a pillow over your head. Or thinking about leaving, and finally managing to drift off, then still staying.

There's no gunfire now. Pushers are limited now to two street corners, near the underpass. It's full of bars now and young people shouting outside all night long. With every glass, their voices grow louder. Sleeping means earplugs and a pillow over your head. Or opening the window and pointless shouting. Or thinking about leaving, not sleeping, that thought gnawing at you. Then still staying.

—

The Home of Words is on the second floor of a building built in the 1930s.

At street level, there's a large window to an old grocery store; the manager installed a grate so people wouldn't sit on the ledge with their drinks. I is directly above this business; he feels the vibrations of the store's refrigerator in his feet, especially on Sundays, when it's quiet. The rest of the week he doesn't notice, though he does hear the bell ring as each customer comes in.

Every day, I enters the Home of Words around dawn and he leaves with the sunset. Sooner during the winter; during the summer around dinnertime, following the rhythms of the sun. I doesn't want to see the collapsing, the dying of the light.

At lunchtime, he goes out, gets a sandwich at a coffee bar or some pasta at a trattoria. He doesn't talk to anyone; he prefers a place with a TV on, likes to stare into the rectangle of light.

The Home of Words is a two-by-four-meter room. There's a window overlooking the street and a door in front of the stairs. I's name isn't by the doorbell or intercom. No one rings for him because no one knows he's there. If the bell rings, it's for someone else; I never opens to anyone.

In the Home of Words there's a table, a desk chair, and an armchair.

Behind the desk is a chalkboard that Wife gave I: in chalk, she wrote, "For your words." Wife's words and her clean, delicate handwriting blanket his shoulders.

The walls are white, bare, with only nail holes and frames of absence. From the life before in that place.

I has done nothing to remove these traces. Within the frames, the light has drawn on the wall; the past watches I, and I can watch the past.

The largest holes probably once held up a shelf. Or two—one above the other. I hasn't put up a shelf or brought many books; the few books he does have are piled on the table; these books are always changing.

He does have a lot of notebooks, though: small engagement books, eighty pages, grid or ruled paper; it doesn't matter. White eraser curls appear between the pages and also on the table, which is black. A slight snowfall, circumscribed, of eliminated words.

The chair by the table is a swivel office chair.

I usually sits turned toward the window, staring off at the building across the street. If someone appears at the window and looks his way, I turns back to his computer screen.

When he steps inside the Home of Words, he takes off his shoes and arranges them side by side, near the door. If it's summer, he also removes his socks; he folds them and tucks them where his feet just were.

When he slips off his shoes and turns on his computer screen, I moves into a place where Wife doesn't exist.

Every day, he grabs hold of one end of the string of words he sees on the computer screen, holding on, sliding down, bare toes pointed at the white wall of his monitor, until he disappears, below, into the rectangle of light.

And what he sees when the light takes him, I doesn't speak of this to Wife or Little Girl; honestly, he wouldn't know what to say.

All he knows is he comes back at sunset: he grabs hold of the string of words and, pointing his toes at the wall, he pulls himself up meter by meter. Until he reaches the surface, and reappears, beyond the glowing rectangle of the computer monitor, in his office.

—

And what I sees during those hours, seven minutes away from the Home where he lives with Family, perhaps all that remains of what he sees are traces left in his expression.

In the evening, when he sits down at the table for dinner with Wife and Little Girl, they don't ask him what happened during his day. Wife only asks how it went, and he says, "Well"; then they talk about other things.

Wife would like to ask more but knows this is what's most dangerous. She knows the only thing she can do is wait; that one day, when it's all done and he lets her read it, Wife will understand and redistribute everything, divided into each silent past dinner.

But day after day, she can only try to decipher that expression I wears at the table. And try to understand if something is shifting inside, if something irreparable has occurred; if there's a space for her, too, somewhere. Or if he's already moved someplace different, coming home now only to sleep.

6

Home Beneath the Mountain, 1983

While a fortress, it's nestled on the fourth floor of a recently constructed condominium building. I's last name is by the intercom, in the same typeface as the others on the push-button panel. It's the third name on the right, and pressing the button gets you in to a ringing sound. Inside is a family that Father has locked away and that only appears now and then at the window.

I is eight; if he could, he'd look outside forever.

The location: a town of a thousand in the foothills to the Alps. Nearly eight hundred kilometers from the Underground Home, the greatest distance still within the country's borders.

The condominium is part of a residential complex, its construction announced years before the complex was actually built. Three mustard-colored buildings, surrounded on three sides by flower beds and three signs posted saying: "Trampling the flowers is strictly prohibited." On the fourth side of the complex is a modest-sized parking lot. From here, access to the complex is down a series of cobblestone paths leading to the front door.

The Home Beneath the Mountain consists of a kitchen and two

rooms. These rooms are off a central hallway. At the end of the hall, always closed, is the pebble-glass door to the bathroom.

Once inside, the kitchen is the first room to the right. On the same side, down the hall, is the dining room. The furniture in both rooms is from a local factory specializing in alpine furnishings. The kitchen table, the sideboard, and also the couch, two armchairs, and wardrobe are massive wood pieces engraved with a floral pattern.

There's a small balcony off the kitchen. It faces a planted field. Past the field is the road, blacktop not visible. On the right, you can make out the cemetery with its solid, low walls and the path bordered by cypresses.

On the left, the paper mill's smokestacks blow clouds into the sky. Although marginal in the topography around here, the paper mill is the area's driving force guaranteeing employment. It also raises the testosterone level of teenage boys with all the porn magazines left out by the dumpsters. It will be out there, with no imaginative effort, that I will have his first conscious ejaculation, a release, a jolt in the lower abdomen, without even touching himself.

But that's not now—that's in a few years—for now the paper mill is only billowing, blinking, and burning, and I is a little boy watching it being swallowed up by smoke in the background. Often, he's watching the older boys out on their bikes along the main road, groups of three or four, shouting and standing up on their pedals, excited to be reaching their destination, and the promise of photos of breasts and genitals, stained with rain, mud, and sperm. And he also watches these boys riding back slowly—hours later—tires buzzing, chains still.

—

I's room is across from the dining room. A large room with a wardrobe that has three plain doors. The bunk bed, a nice display of the floral pattern, is to the left as he enters.

I sleeps on the top bunk, protected by a massive wood headboard. Every night he scrambles up the ladder and climbs into bed. Sister is in the lower bunk.

The window looks onto a balcony that juts out over the complex's flower bed. Not far off, looms the mountain.

The dining room is Father's room, the same way the kitchen pertains to Mother, defining a clear social hierarchy and areas of specialization. Father only enters the kitchen to eat; Mother, the dining room, only to make the bed.

After dinner, in fact, the dining room transforms to a private room. The couch with the flower pattern expels the queen-size bed. The armchairs are set by the window and the TV goes on, with Father and Mother watching from under the covers. What you see if you go in there after dinner is a normal bedroom.

I understands that metamorphoses exist, that the universe can capsize at any moment. I accepts that his world can be subverted, quashed, if Father chooses. He accepts that disappearances are a fact of nature.

For him it's enough to retreat into the carapace of his room, climb over the railing, and stare up at the ceiling, like a turtle staring inside its own shell.

In the Home Beneath the Mountain, there are no telephones because Father needs his rest. That's why it's always silent, while in the upstairs and downstairs apartments, a phone is always ringing.

Once a week, Mother will leave with a handful of coins and

go to the phone booth three hundred meters away. These coins for phone calls she saves up in an ashtray near the sets of keys in the entryway. When Mother returns from her phone call, she tells them that Relatives say hello.

The missing phone is the fence colliding with Grandma's and Relatives' phone calls. It's where Father has walled in I's family.

Walled-in alive, the family stays safe.

Father is free to rest easy.

Mother sets the change from shopping aside so she can call.

7

Turtle's Home, 1968

THERE'S NOT MUCH SPACE, BUT it doesn't feel cramped. It's conceived for a single tenant, a studio of sorts, with the bare necessities.

Only one entrance, at the front.

From here, Turtle observes the world; from here, more often, she withdraws.

Toward the back are two windows, always open, where light enters and legs exit. Other openings appear closer to the front, on either side.

The ceiling is vaulted, imposing, in spite of the Home's reduced size. The openings—front and back—project everything Turtle passes onto the vault. The world is everything that winds up projected onto the ceiling. When Turtle moves, the projection changes: the vault becomes a screen; her home is a traveling movie theater.

The floor, like all the other surfaces, is a bony material. About ten tiles, though they seem to be a single casting.

Austere but not cold, elegant with imperfections.

Turtle doesn't so much walk on that floor as stretch out there.

What she walks across is outside, where she leaves her footprints.

The interior is somewhat plain. With the acoustics of a cave: the noise of the world remains trapped inside, entering through the windows and spreading. Little by little, the sound grows weaker, slowly leaking out.

Inside her home, thunder rumbles and echoes on and on. Rain makes her apartment a living hell. Every drop becomes a drumroll.

Viewed from the outside, Turtle's Home is a private dwelling. One story, no upstairs or downstairs neighbors, no intrusions. No foundation, sitting on the ground.

The roof is made up of sixty dark inlaid tiles.

An outdoor bathroom.

Turtle's Home is also her tomb.

She drags it behind her with every step. While alive, she lives there.

She won't have to move when she dies.

Turtle's Home exists in the same urban context as the Underground Home. Rome, the 1960s fading, coming to a close.

But Turtle has only just arrived; she doesn't know anything yet.

Grandma (not Grandma yet, only Father's mother, and Father still only a son) found her in the grass, in a nearby park. She thought Turtle was a stone, but then she saw her moving: slowly, of course, but moving enough to erase any doubt. When Grandma picked her up to look more closely, Turtle shut herself back up inside her home, but first she saw the sky.

She appeared again as she heard Grandma speaking, asking her where she came from, why she was there, where she was going. Seeing that face speaking to her from so close, Turtle trusted her, which hasn't always been the case.

Turtle was still small, she fit in one hand; Grandma carried her in her palm the entire way back to the front door of the Underground Home.

The whole trip, Grandma spoke to her; they met some women, spent a short time together. They all tried to touch Turtle's head, but she stayed hidden.

Just to be safe, she stayed inside the rest of the flight.

Then they went down the stairs to the Underground Home, and Grandma opened the door, turned on the lights, and went out to the courtyard opposite the kitchen and set Turtle on the ground, and she ran behind the first pot. Jasmine would grow there, that Grandma planted a few weeks before.

Rather than buildings, Turtle now sees flowerpots, the cement blocks she walks across, the green rubber tube that sometimes spouts a jet of water over the flowers, the tree trunk, a dark bucket.

$$8$$

Home of Sex, 1991

The Home of Sex is a corner apartment, on the fourth floor of a 1950s apartment building at the edge of a small town with metropolitan ambitions. Oriented toward the street, on this side there's the kitchen and living-room/dining-room combo, with a balcony. On the other side, Virgin Girl's room, her parents' room, and the bathroom. The décor is modern; the kitchen has a dishwasher, plus a microwave, the first one I's ever seen. The dishwasher is noisy and heats up the kitchen, so the family closes this door after meals. Every room has a TV, except for Virgin Girl's room.

The living-room/dining-room combo has a leather couch and an easy chair, plus a massive wood table—plain, devoid of floral emblems—which they use if they entertain in the evening. During the day, it's Virgin Girl's desk: she leaves her third-year high school textbooks and notebooks on this table.

Nearly every afternoon, I bikes over. It's not more than ten or fifteen minutes from the Home Beneath the Mountain. He wears his backpack filled with textbooks. On the hills up to Virgin Girl's home, I feels the entire weight of his burden, so he stands up on the pedals.

—

On the dining room table, Virgin Girl and I discover ecstasy and the bewilderment brought on by sex. Virgin Girl stretches out over her books, opens her legs, lets her skirt ride up her hips. At this point, I penetrates her, clothed, standing at the head of the table. The door to the room is closed, and neither one of them thinks it might open. And it doesn't, but they also wouldn't notice if it did, in their frenzy.

Virgin Girl's slender body lies on a bed of asymptotes, pie charts, Cicero, Dante passages. What I views as he climbs onto the table, lies down over her, and continues enthusiastically thrusting. Cicero, Newton, Pythagoras, they watch as his face twists in a spasm.

Then the two change places: I rolls onto his back on the table and waits for Virgin Girl to straddle him, squeaking with pleasure, her knees crumpling their homework.

When they're done, I slips out from under, pulls the rubber off with a smack. Then they go back to studying, flushed, their breathing slowing down, finding its own pace.

Sometimes Virgin Girl, not satisfied, begins again: she disappears under the table, gets down on all fours and takes his erection in her mouth. I remains composed, doesn't drop his pen on his notebook. It's only when he ejaculates that he drops his pen and groans, fist striking his notebook. Afterwards, Virgin Girl returns to the surface, sits down, smiling, not saying a word, and goes back to writing as if nothing's happened.

Virgin Girl and I aren't going out, and they never speak to each other with affection or make any promises. They're complementary bodies that couple every afternoon.

When I leaves by early evening, Virgin Girl clears the table, takes her books and notebooks to her room, then sets the table for dinner. She spreads out a white tablecloth, arranges the silverware by the plates, puts the glasses up to the right. She doesn't think for one instant about what's underneath, the traces of her secrets conserved in the wood.

9

Family's Self-Propelling Home, 2008

NOT AN AUTONOMOUS DWELLING PER se, though resistant to the cold and other bad weather. Self-propelling with a motor, but that doesn't matter, and neither do all its kilometers. A dwelling that's an extension of Family's Home.

Technically, a Fiat Panda, white, with a flirtatious flurry of stickers, one of them a faded baby sticker. Compact, geometric, square-lined, straight-nosed: one of the many heirs to Italy's mass-produced tin cans which then canned the new family of the late '50s, happy, satisfied, each new family alike and headed for the coast. Models from the '80s, not flashy, utterly reliable, and with an abundance of spare parts.

Some paint missing around the headlights, but otherwise, not too bad. Their regular mechanic reassures them: the Self-Propelling Home, it would seem, plans to go on forever. A source of great comfort to mechanics: with the hood propped open, they take in the sight of the motor as though gazing over an extremely sensible landscape. Everything is visible; everything is familiar; everything can be attended to. No electronic control unit, meaning no religious frenzy of maintenance. The last spark of enlightenment left on the market.

—

The Self-Propelling Home is where Family truly takes shape. It was their true incubator from the beginning, the depository that allowed—allows—for their survival.

Imperfect at birth, the Self-Propelling Home has been kept alive by science when nature would have killed it off. First the assembly of the two disconnected parts—I on one side and Wife + Little Girl on the other, not tied by blood—then came the sutures. A successful first surgery, no recorded glitches or infections.

The next step was potentially the most lethal—to which almost all family organisms (modified like theirs) succumb: survival in an outside environment, exposed to threats from the world. The Self-Propelling Home performs a very delicate function: it's the hyperbaric chamber for Family in its postoperative phase, the sealed, carefully sanitized space where Family waged its first struggles to survive. Intensive treatment the first year, then downshifting but never entirely abandoning the piece of equipment.

That's why, in this initial phase, I + Wife and Little Girl always go around shut up inside this metal container with wheels. Anyone watching them roll by can see that they're in a delicate place, on a very thin ridge between certain death and artificial life. Wife and I in front—I at the wheel, Wife beside him.

They never spend less than two hours a day inside their incubator. Traveling all around the city, but more often, slipping onto the two-lane bypass headed for the Alps or else to the sea. Trips, both long and scenic, make the treatment less burdensome: not to mention, the outside, if it's nice, is like an inside with the added pleasure of enjoying it while seated. The surrounding countryside, the mirrored water seen from the turn onto the provincial road, is the perfect setting for programmed cell regeneration, meaning, the metamorphosis from I + Wife and Little Girl to Family, period, full stop.

What's happening inside can be seen through the windows, which is basically zip. Moods forming in a closed space, brought on, circulating from what's said. The temperature inside the Self-Propelling Home—68 to 78 degrees—is necessary in order to trigger the desired cellular response for this type of surgery. Aside from this, anything goes, munching potato chips, singing, not talking for long stretches, fighting, falling asleep.

Periodically, Wife and I check to see that the treatment's working. This happens at night, at the table or in front of the TV or out on a walk.

I wants to see immediate results.

Wife is far more patient.

Little Girl believes whoever's the most persuasive at the time.

On some nights it does seem to be happening—there are glimpses of Family—and Wife and I make love into the late hours.

Other nights, though, nothing seems to be happening; I sees the trench between their separate sides, Wife and Little Girl at a distance—and not a trace of Family, just a bad reaction.

When this occurs, I goes out for a walk, wanders like a cat through Turin, sticking close to the buildings, appearing in the lit doorways, darting into the shadows cast by the streetlamps, between the parked cars.

Out on the street, he looks inside the lit apartment; from his face, it's hard to tell how he's feeling—free or rejected—but this is usually clear from his stride. If he sees the Self-Propelling Home in the paid parking lot, between the blue painted lines, it's out of the corner of his eye, and left at that.

10

Relatives' Home, 1985

RELATIVES' HOME IS ON THE third floor of a six-story building. This building was designed and constructed in the late '60s, like the rest of the district.

It's three kilometers as the crow flies from the Underground Home, headed toward Fiumicino Airport. A straightforward, half hour stroll through the hills. The buildings of the area, when you arrive, are fairly uniform, tending toward orange. Sometimes yellow, with gray railings.

At a glance, this might be the same neighborhood, but meter by meter, the color shifts, the slightest details alter; by the end of this walk, past the main street, all resemblance stops. No more park, no domes, no monuments, no pre-Christian ruins.

The historic center isn't even a thought now—this is the center now, the only possible center, like all the other suburbs. The oldest inscriptions on stone were done in spray paint, and date back to the '83 championship.

Relatives' Home is mainly a hallway; at the end of this hallway, Relatives sit around all day. You see them when you come in, shrunk in perspective. Sometimes one Relative will separate from the background and come meet the new arrival, will slowly increase in size on the approach. And at the door, will be on a 1:1 scale.

Relatives' Home consists of only a few rooms. A dining-room/living-room combo halfway down the hall; here there's a round table with one leaf, a couch, a sideboard for the holiday plates and glasses, and a medium-sized TV on a stand. When not in use, this room stays closed, the rolling shutters always pulled down.

The rest of the apartment is made up of a long, narrow, modular kitchen; a master bedroom with a tall four-season wardrobe reaching the ceiling; and two smaller, nondescript bedrooms where Young Relatives sleep.

The difference between the Young and Old Relatives' rooms: the former have bulletin boards covered in photos and the latter has photos in silver frames of married couples and Dead Relatives.

I's memories of the Home are vague and intermittent. He remembers, and then those memories dissolve as if they never existed. Then they reappear, flicker, disappear.

Through Father's decree, in fact, Relatives disappear for fairly long periods, sometimes months, sometimes years; in some cases, they disappear forever. The word, "Relatives," is abolished from the lexicon of the Home Beneath the Mountain. Relatives no longer exist, and if Sister and I say that word, Father threatens to abolish them as well.

With this word erased, Relatives disappear from I's mind.

Only Mother, going to the phonebooth with her handful of coins, pronounces this word, and when she comes back, she brings greetings from the entire family. But the day she calls, the thought of Relatives shows on her face, like a black eye. Relatives' warm voice, for Mother, is a punch in the face, a mark lasting for days. During that time, Father won't look at her and waits for the bruise to disappear.

Then it disappears, and Mother thanks Father for allowing her to call. She says her thank you by making Relatives disappear from her thoughts. Otherwise, Father would see them in her eyes. That's why Mother swallows them, squeezing her eyes shut with the effort: she feels them going down her throat, scraping her esophagus, striking her pylorus; they hit her stomach like a rockslide, though on the outside, the crashing of their bones makes no sound.

Relatives are too big, too hard, to grind between her teeth. So Mother consigns them to the flames of hydrochloric acid. Their Home, too. This is her gift to Father every week: Relatives dissolved in her stomach.

There are nights when Mother has a stomachache. Lying in bed, I hears her moaning; sometimes she cries for the pain, and he hears Father, nearby, telling her how to make it go away.

When Mother's moaning gets too loud, Father takes her to the hospital for tests. But they never find anything: there's nothing in her stomach, nothing there.

Mother is good about not leaving a trace of Relatives behind, dissolving them in acid. They slip a tube down her throat and into her stomach. The camera at the end of the tube, every time it goes down, shows everything is empty. Father looks at the results and is satisfied and brings Mother home. If she still cries the next night, they don't return to the hospital.

Father rewards Mother for her good behavior in the bedroom: Sister and I hear the sofa bed hitting the wall and Mother's panting. Stomachaches and sex become a single moan.

Sister rolls over and faces the wall; I pulls the pillow over his head.

After a while, everything's quiet.

This is how Relatives' Home disappears.

Then reappears.

Through Father's decree, Mother takes her coins to the phone-booth to say that after all this time, they'll get to see each other. She returns, trying to hide her joy. Then she packs for them, and Father arranges the bags in the car in a pleasing geometric pattern.

On the trip from Home Beneath the Mountain to Relatives' Home, Mother summarizes Relatives, who they are, what they do, what's happened since they've been gone. It's an eight-hour drive, and Sister and I listen, distracted, watching the cars go by on the highway.

When they're back in Relatives' Home after so much time, usually someone separates off from the end of the hall and moves toward Father, Mother, Sister, and I. Then Relative hugs all four of them and says things and sounds happy.

Sometimes I recognizes these people, other times, no. He recognizes this space as if remembering a different space: not that it's new to him, but it's a matter of connecting the heart and the sense of smell and leaving the brain out of the equation.

One after another, Relatives hug them, especially Sister and I, the children. I answers all their questions because this is included with Father's decree. Sister stays quiet, turned nearly always toward I while Relatives talk among themselves.

I tries to tell them apart because they all look alike. And they also look like Mother. And they look like I, too, which Father can't forgive, just like he can't forgive Mother, and Relatives most of all.

Then the rolling shutters go up in the dining room, the holiday tablecloth goes on the table, and they start setting the table for everyone. Sister and I help, though they don't know where to find the silverware, glasses, or plates.

During this meal, I turns to the others and calls them Relatives, because he's supposed to. They keep saying how happy they are and that he and Sister are Relatives, too. I looks at Father to make sure this is correct, but Father is silent; he wants to know what I will say. So I says nothing, just smiles, embarrassed that he looks like them. But if the doctors put a tube down his throat, down to his stomach, the camera would show that Relatives don't exist. Or maybe they do, maybe they do exist—so it's better not to take any chances, better not to try, not to let that probe look around, just to keep swallowing, swallowing again.

11

Prisoner's Home, 1978

IF I CRAWLED INSIDE THE TV's rectangle of light, in the dining room of the Underground Home, he'd go down a long hallway that no one sees.

At the other end of that hallway, inside the Home where he's locked up against his will, Prisoner would see a baby coming toward him in a diaper and tank top.

Slowly, perhaps not even aware of this man watching him, I would reach Prisoner. At this point he'd have to see him. Perhaps he'd grab onto the man's leg, to pull himself to his feet.

Prisoner would pick him up.

Perhaps, more likely, I would just look at Prisoner and keep his distance.

Prisoner's Home is about four square meters in size. A single room, no windows. A simple bed, against a wall; a cot. Toward the back of the room, a small table and a wood chair.

Perhaps I would find Prisoner sitting at the table and writing something on a sheet of paper.

Or sitting on the cot. Or on the floor, his back against the wall.

There's a bare bulb hanging from the ceiling; it's lit but shows nothing. The bulb reveals that without it, there'd be only darkness and loud, steady breathing.

Prisoner doesn't know where his home is located. He only knows that everything ends here, that his world finishes in this cubic volume.

He doesn't know that beyond a window, there's a park with an abandoned villa; that trees wave over Rome; that it's early spring.

He doesn't know whose heels hit the floor above, but he recognizes every vibration.

He doesn't know that his home is inside another, which, in turn, is in an apartment building, which is inside a larger home, which is Italy.

If I slipped into the TV's rectangle of light, in the dining room of the Underground Home, perhaps he'd arrive too late, and leaving, would only find the cot, and not Prisoner.

He'd crawl across that empty space, hands and knees on the floor, nothing else to see.

And perhaps he wouldn't even hear it, down in the cellar: the gunshots.

12

Home of Adultery, 1994

It's a provincial town, indistinguishable in Northern Italy, a town like any other town like any other town like any other provincial town. Outside Turin, it's endlessly provincial in every direction.

The Home of Adultery is mainly a window and a field of vision. The field of vision is from the outside looking inside, at a diagonal, from below to up above. Above is Woman with the Wedding Ring's window; below, at street level, is I, nineteen years old, looking straight up at the fourth floor.

Between the street and the window, a column. No, more of a pillar, concrete, so a mix of cement, gravel, water, and sand. He's on the opposite side of the street from that window, and standing in a portico. In a place where he escapes notice, this place of his daily stakeout. The point of contact is his right shoulder, half his face poking out.

I knows every detail of this pillar. Any new graffiti at all, he sees it. There's not much, most of it in spray paint: anarchy in black, intimacy in red. I Love You, or Fuck You, Always or Never Again, that sort of thing.

—

The window—like all the others in the building, painted frame, standard-sized, two-paneled, opening out—is the designated mouth, the spokesperson for Woman with the Wedding Ring: it's the window that talks to I from above, that instructs and gives his wait meaning. It's the mouth of the building, the love oracle, the frame that will predict how long he must yearn.

The window speaks, and it is this that keeps I where he is, looking up.

The language the window speaks, addressing him, is composed of fabric and geometry. An orthogonal alphabet that anticipates horizontal and vertical movements. From above to below, through the green PVC rolling shutter; from left to right with the white tulle curtain.

Woman with the Wedding Ring's words, that only I can decipher, are an encrypted combination of the x- and y-axes.

Vertical for practical communication, horizontal for emotional.

Y-axis: rolling shutter halfway down, Husband at home; up a third of the way, Husband about to leave; all the way up, just out the door. Rolling shutter down, we're out, don't bother waiting.

X-axis: curtain closed, I love you but we're sitting here; curtain pulled back about ten centimeters, I love you and you'll see me here soon, so keep an eye out; curtain halfway open, I love you, I'm trying to get the Twins to go to sleep; curtain open—entirely pulled to the right—I love you, I'm going out but I'll be back soon, and we'll be together, we'll close this curtain and finally make love.

Right shoulder against the pillar, chin raised toward the window, I translates what that oracle has to say. If it's good news, meaning, the time has come for him to enter the Home of Adultery, he'll feel a shiver from his ankles to his groin and he'll swell inside his pants. He slides his hand into his pocket and feels his erection. He swallows, trying to reduce the pressure on his temples.

If nothing happens, if the oracular frame says only to wait, wait without end, if the wait continues with no shift in the two directions this language contemplates, I, in contrast, feels everything being pulled downward. Hope is a grave, dragging chin and eyes down, toward the ground; even sex withers, is dead weight.

Then the raising of the rolling shutter, even after the most grueling of waits, suddenly lifts I's mood. The roller spinning, the traction raising the shutter, also pulls up I's chin and penis, both going back to staring at the window. Everything is proudly antigravitational once more.

And now I knows it's only a matter of seconds. He can shift his gaze downward, to the front door. It will open and Husband will step out, a leather folder under his arm, a tie, hair combed, wedding ring on his finger. He'll head left, then turn soon after.

He, Husband, doesn't know that as soon as he turns, someone across the street will step out from behind a pillar. And even if he saw this person, more than likely Husband wouldn't be suspicious: it's only a boy with a backpack, his Walkman on.

The boy will cross the street, disappear through the main door Husband just walked out of. On the fourth floor, through the abscissas of curtains, the window will say that there's nothing more to see now. And for a couple of hours, it will stay quiet.

13

Home of the Radio, 1999

FROM THE BALCONY ON THE eighth floor, there's a clear view of the mountains. It's August, but the mountaintops are white.

Below is the road leading to the highway to Milan: a two-way street, four lanes, but lately, empty of traffic. And there are hardly any parked cars, just a couple, which will stay all month.

The building is early twentieth-century, a parallelepiped, the lower floors blackened from exhaust fumes. Some graffiti, with only one word legible, "Pigs," which is partly covered by a giant, purple phallus that serves as an exclamation point. The scrotum, detached, is the dot at the bottom, making it exclaim.

The rest of the block is buildings of the same height; mainly, eight stories. The effect is of a single, uninterrupted building headed for the edge of Turin, quashed only by perspective. It does stop suddenly, though, collapses after the last building, into fields, then low houses, everything closer to the ground, up to the airport further on, and then, only sky.

Nothing like the distance separating I, who leans over the balcony rail, from the pavement. His head is twenty meters from the street; the road dominates everything around it. Not much around here, these endless midsummer days, but it's a good spot to take in the Alps.

I is about to turn twenty-four and is at his first job; he's chopped off his college ponytail for the occasion. His hair is short, a normal cut, sideburns trimmed. He still writes poetry but doesn't look like it.

The Home of the Radio is an apartment like any other in the building but without beds, bedrooms, or a kitchen. It does have those rooms, meaning, four along a hallway. Two are set up as radio studios, three microphones on a round table plus an ashtray, headphones hanging on a hook, concert posters on the walls. In the back, a mixer console, an overhead microphone.

The walls are covered in gray foam-rubber panels that absorb sound and also cigarette smoke, which slowly, steadily, seeps out over the course of the day.

There's a broadcast going on in the first studio. A man and woman pretend to argue, chatter. Topics: pets, swimsuits, summer activities, nuclear power, daycare. He keeps announcing the musical piece swelling in the background; she complains that they never get to talk.

It's a recorded broadcast—there's no one in the studio. Just empty chairs, an open window, the voices of a man and a woman filling the room, and the ads. And I sitting there, smoking; then he goes back to the second studio.

The second studio is like the first, only smaller; every hour, a few minutes before the hour's up, I slips on a set of headphones and reads the news.

For three minutes, so about five news items that he chooses off the printout from the fax machine sitting on a desk in the corner. These items are off a long roll of paper. There's a box under the desk, and the paper unravels into this. Over the weekend, the box overflows, the paper spreading over the floor, then stretching into the hallway, the facts on the paper dragging across the tiles. Reality is a wriggling paper snake.

Nothing happens in the summer. It's the tradition in Turin, to keep time with the nothing scheduled for the Fiat factories. Although divested, Lingotto still determines the city's marking of time.

Which means that every hour, for three minutes, I reads the nothing divided into news items. This nothing then leaks from car radios, into stores, the few offices that are open, worksites, prisons, overheated kitchens. Fan blades strike this nothing and it swirls about the rooms, cools down for people gasping for air.

Every hour I returns to see if the roll has produced anything else for him to slap together for the news. From the hall, he can already hear the printer pins scratching the paper, line by line.

He watches the paper snake slither to the floor. If he didn't come check it, if he left for a week, the snake would reach the balcony and slide through the rails, down along the walls, then fill up the city.

But I keeps coming every day.

Every hour he tears off five pieces.

At the end of the day when he leaves the Home of the Radio, he knows, during the night, that reality will always spill out onto the parquet floor. But he doesn't care—it doesn't matter to him now. Every night, he just shuts the door, steps onto the elevator, and doesn't give it another thought.

I doesn't ask much from August. He has a girlfriend, they have fun, sex, and that's enough to wade through the rest of the summer.

At night they sometimes sleep out on her balcony, are lulled to sleep by the sporadic, reassuring suburban traffic.

The last room in the Home of the Radio is the bathroom. The bathtub is partway filled with water. In this water, soaking, is a turtle: the turtle is owned by I's employer, the radio station manager.

I has his instructions before leaving. The turtle food is kept under the news desk; a spoonful every morning; a couple on the weekend; don't ever forget.

The turtle soaking in the bathtub is fairly large, and still growing. The station manager had set the turtle in I's arms to see how he handled this. Of course he handled it well; he smiled at the turtle, and she tucked her head inside her shell.

Then his boss put the turtle back in the water and added some toy boats to the tub.

Now that his boss is on vacation, he calls regularly to ask how the turtle is doing.

When I goes into the bathroom, he talks to her. He sits on the toilet, rests his elbows on his knees and peers into the tub.

The turtle churns her feet and swims to meet him, kicking up spurts of dirty water. She throws herself into crawling up the ceramic sides of the tub, but after a few tries, scratching the enamel, she slides back down in the water.

I changes the water in the tub twice a week; day after day, it grows browner and browner and the turtle swims in her own feces; and the bathroom grows more and more oppressive.

I pulls out the bathtub plug and the water drains.

He uses a spatula to scrape the shit into a bag specifically for this purpose.

Then he kneels beside the tub, points the handheld shower-head, and sprays the turtle; she stretches her head, opens her mouth for the water, a festival of spraying water over her shell.

Every day I lifts the turtle out of the tub and lets her loose to wander around the Home of the Radio; she's sluggish, takes a few steps, then stops.

Sometimes she comes into the studio while I is reading the news; she pushes in under his chair. It's hot out, and I is always barefoot: she looks for his big toe and comes closer.

They study each other. If she touches the toe, it moves.

When the turtle enters the studio at a decent clip, I notices: he hears a banging in his headphones as he speaks. They're the thuds of her plastron on the floor—amplified—spreading by radio over the entire city.

14

Underground Home, 1975

THE POLYPHONY OF THE WORLD is far away, to put it simply. Inside the amniotic sac, I is a marginal lump in relation to the large belly Mother displays as she walks around the apartment or through the streets of Rome. According to the manuals, he already has ears. Actually, he has almost everything, everything for life; actually, he's ready, fully equipped, though it's still too soon: life would kill him off before it gave him the illusion it gives to all, the illusion of pardon, of granting him eternity.

So I hears, from within his first true dwelling, set inside another, at the top of a city hill. What he hears is pure hypothesis, but more than likely includes road traffic, ambulances, Grandma's hoarseness, the roaring of water in the sink or shower, domestic clatter. Of course there's Father's voice, or at least the vibration of his voice; like everyone else, Father probably leans over the closed door of his wife's bellybutton and allows his vocal cords to vibrate in greeting. I understands Sister, the pressure on the placental ceiling when she climbs into Mother's arms. He understands the primitive percussion of Turtle, the drumroll of preparing to enter the world. And added to these, perhaps weekly, the booming of the cannon firing on Rome. All the rest is Mother, his first environment, his sensory organ, his primordial refuge.

The rest, what's wading in I's first sea, what he intercepts, might be searched for by sifting through the cerebral cortex, which might reveal something else entirely from what's been hypothesized here. It doesn't really matter. What's certain is that in this phase everything I perceives is perceived head-down, in an upended world.

But that's not the point. The point is the scream, what's happening inside now, that starts in the silence of the Underground Home, and then becomes Mother's piercing, panicked scream, Father's excited chatter, Grandma's voice that draws everything together into a decision, to call the hospital.

It's not a matter of water breaking, not evolutionary unpreparedness. It's Mother vomiting in the dining room, mostly blood and sputum, and blood between her legs as she touches herself, holds up her hands to see, and lets out a scream that shatters the still of the neighborhood, cracking the sky in Monteverde. What's happening inside her belly is hard to say, but they fear the worst for I, head down in his final slide. And he perceives this, as a roar, thunder, nothing, who can say.

The rest happens very quickly, Mother at home, on the bed, Grandma, raising Mother's nightgown, better to maneuver, shouting at her son to keep quiet, to look after Sister, only telling Mother, "It'll be all right, there's nothing to be afraid of," and meanwhile wiping the blood off her thighs with a piece of cloth, petting her hair, telling her belly, "Little one." Finally, the stretcher, the siren through the neighborhood, the hospital lobby, then after the drama, the final joy, the regular heartbeat, the baby still alive, a gorgeous autumn in Rome, the abrupt cobalt sky of early winter.

And then, the return to underground, Turtle waiting, standing guard. Mother put to bed, Grandma keeping an eye on her, intermittent sleep and feeble smiles. Grandma handles everything else, the shopping, lunch for her son, lettuce for the turtle out in the yard, baby food for Sister. There's still dried blood on the dining-room floor that Grandma, smoking, not thinking much about it, wipes away with a sponge.

Above, on the table, what likely brought on the scream, the hypothetical fuse that set off the explosion, random, pure coincidence, laid out as evidence: an open newspaper, the photos of Murdered Poet, face mangled, soles of his shoes toward the lens, in his undershirt, lying in the dirt. Grandma closes the paper, sets it on the couch, an old domestic habit.

15

Home of the Wardrobe, 2004

IT'S ON THE EIGHTH FLOOR of a late nineteenth-century building in Turin's historic center; Wife and Little Girl live there, though Wife isn't wife yet; she's only mother at this point.

She knows nothing of I; he's not a hypothesis but might be hoped for.

Getting to the apartment requires going up seven flights of stairs, but no one ever does; people use the long, thin elevator instead; the maximum capacity, according to the plaque, is three.

From the balcony, you can see the Alps.

The mountain range, seen from up there, is the lower arch of a set of dentures. They're crooked teeth, not aligned; all told, they look unkempt, only white in spots, uncared for; they needed braces in their childhood, in the Oligocene epoch.

You can't see the upper arch—it's too high—the mouth yawns open. Every night the upper arch comes down and joins the lower arch; a slow descent, light gradually cut off in the windows. Then the mouth shuts like a hatch, and the apartment where Wife and Little Girl live is thrown into darkness.

Then every morning, the mouth slowly opens again, and day returns inside.

There are two rooms plus two niches. The first niche is the kitchen, just enough space for someone at the stovetop, and also a miniature window. The other niche is the bathroom: the toilet, shower, and small washing machine are tiles in a composition unconcerned with bodies in motion.

The first of the two rooms is a multipurpose living room: dining room, game and homework room for Little Girl, office for Wife. The second room is a bedroom that Wife has turned into two rooms with a wardrobe as a partition.

On one side of the wardrobe is Wife's bed, queen-size, though only one body sleeps here. On the other side is Little Girl's bed.

The wardrobe is small, certainly not a wall. More like an onstage scene-divider. There's a door on each side so Wife and Little Girl can have mirrored existences, each in her own space. Sometimes they both pull open a wardrobe door, on both sides, at the same moment, without speaking; in that simultaneous gesture and the way they resemble each other, they don't seem like two people but two different epochs of the same personal history.

It's never been the case that Wife wanted Little Girl to sleep with her. It's always been the case that Little Girl has objected, staking her claim to the empty side of the bed.

Wife says it doesn't matter—just because a warm body's not lying there doesn't mean it's not being used. So the rule stays: "Each to her own room."

For years, every night they each get in position on their half of the field, on either side of the wardrobe.

They pull back the covers and tuck their legs and bare feet under; they shift into position. Both with their head on the pillow: Wife, the back of her neck against it—pillow propped up, book in hand—Little Girl, on her right cheek, turned toward the wardrobe that separates her from her mother.

After an initial, concentrated silence, Little Girl tosses her first word over the wardrobe, to the other side. Then she waits for it to come back, modified by her mother's breath. If it's too late in returning, she sends another over until it reappears above the wardrobe and descends over her bed like a winged word. Little Girl strikes it, sends it back, imagines her mother catching it.

Sometimes Wife is distracted or sleepy, settling into her first dream, and soon her bed is littered with Little Girl's fallen words.

After too many of them, she usually wakes up and tosses them back.

This always goes on at least a half hour. The words Little Girl throws over at night are her largest of the day; every hour they've grown a little more, beginning when she woke up. Sometimes they're heavy, and Wife can feel all of Little Girl's effort to hurl them over. So when she sees them coming, she catches them and tries to empty them of everything they hold.

She does this task in her nightgown, with her fingertip: she pokes holes in her daughter's words and empties them, lightens them. So when she sends them back again, they float over the wardrobe like soap bubbles.

Before she goes to sleep, Wife slips across to Little Girl's half of the field and turns off the light and arranges her daughter's body on the mattress.

INISTERO DELLE FINANZE

REZIONE GENERALE DEL CATASTO E DEI SERVIZI TECNICI ERARIALI

Lire 20

NUOVO CATASTO EDILIZIO URBANO

(R. DECRETO LEGGE 13 APRILE 1939, N. 657)

Planimetria dell'immobile situato nel Comune di _______________________

Ditta _______________________

Allegata alla dichiarazione presentata all'Ufficio Tecnico Erariale di _______________________

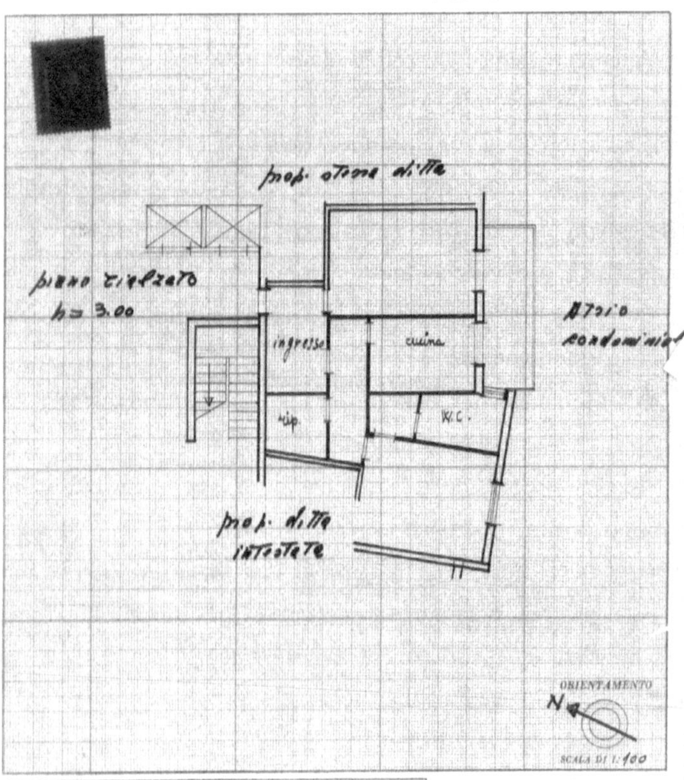

SPAZIO RISERVATO PER LE ANNOTAZIONI D'UFFICIO

DATA

PROT. N°

Compilata dal Geometra _______________________

Iscritto all'Albo dei Geometri (n° 1644)

della Provincia di _______________________

DATA

Firma

16

Underground Home, 2013

TURTLE MOVES ABOUT IN A very small part of the cement yard; she barely leaves her corner. If she does, it's for a lonely little sortie, a pensive, fleeting half circle. She finds greens lying right beside her hiding place behind the flowerpot. She waits until no one's there, then harpoons the lettuce leaf with a clawed toe and draws it closer. And grinds it in her beak.

In a couple of hours, she finishes and retreats, and everything goes back to the emptiness from before.

Turtle doesn't go inside the Underground Home, and no one invites her in, either. The only thing the couple who lives there ever gives her is lettuce. Hard to say if they're the ones who don't interact with her, or if Turtle rejects them. What is certain: it's wall against wall. Unlike Grandma, Occupants only use the cement yard for hanging out the wash. Once a week a banner stretches out of underwear, socks, and pants, and by the next day, it's already gone.

Otherwise, Occupants are nearly always shut up inside. No one sings anymore; no one shouts; no music floats into the cement yard and disappears into the blue square of the sky.

—

Earlier, for five weeks, there was a din of air hammers, drills, and circular saws. Turtle watched as her yard filled with a heap of rubble. A sink sat enthroned at the top for a while. Then everything disappeared. During those weeks of construction, Turtle switched corners to avoid being crushed. Every night, she came out and traveled around the ruins, the sole survivor of a collapsed empire.

Every morning, a young man in coveralls would feed her. He talked to her, picked her up and held her close, at eye level. He wore a baseball cap and had a wild, ragged beard. He brought his finger close to her face so she'd trust him, and she did. Not just for the greens he gave her, but also for his laughter. And for the radio they listened to while her world was collapsing.

Then they washed out the courtyard with a pressure sprayer, and the young man left with a last weary smile.

And Occupants arrived, with their laundry line.

Every time she hears the kitchen window open, Turtle retreats into her carapace. From there she watches Occupants' feet take their few necessary steps. Other than the laundry, for the bag of garbage.

But there are new feet now, and Occupants' feet move to the middle of the cement yard. They ask the other feet for their opinion, what they think about the renovation work done on the apartment. The new feet seem confused: there's more hesitation than words, as if they're embarrassed.

It's I's voice, coming from those feet. There on the ground, his voice slips inside Turtle's shell, and makes her jolt. The voice apologizes for just barging in, for ringing their bell, he was passing through Rome, he lives in Turin now, he doesn't generally pester people, make demands or whatever.

Occupants sound embarrassed; they don't talk about Grandma; they talk about real estate agents they've known.

Turtle's heart is beating like mad; the percussion is amplified in her speaker-shell. So she pushes out her head. Now she sees six feet heading toward the kitchen, and I's feet turn around one last time before going inside.

Suddenly it's raining. Her shell is a tambourine for the sky to play on. Inside her shell, Turtle listens and doesn't move.

The cannon fires in the distance.

17

Home of the Mattress, 1997

It's a students' apartment. If you couldn't tell by the names handwritten in pen by the intercom, you'd certainly figure it out from the doormat, from the pile of shoes lying there, laced up once and forever more. Men's shoes, clearly, from the size and style, but mostly because they're so dirty. Not that they stink, but the effect is of a locker room. Three pairs in all, though it's hard to distinguish this at first: a unique pile, an irregular mass, a solid made up of uppers and soles. Even the nonathletic shoes—that actually display a kind of social ambition—in this pile, seem more like sneakers.

I's shoes are on the other side of the mat, untied and lined up. They're suede and plainly cheap. Their displacement suggests that I is just visiting; their presence points back to the pile. When I leaves, the group of shoes will unite once more, with nothing out of sync.

The apartment has an entryway that ends once you step inside and into the kitchen, where there's a pale blue Formica table, four unmatched chairs, and against the wall, a veneer counter and pots stacked on the range top. In the sink, a pile of dishes in dirty, somewhat soapy water. On the back wall, a window overlooking an internal courtyard and a few bicycles.

To the right when you enter is the bathroom: it runs alongside the kitchen. Terracotta-colored floor tiles, green-tiled walls. The toilet on the back wall crouches like a chimera. Behind the bathroom door (tall, wood), three bathrobes hanging on hooks. By the sink, a snarl of desolate towels.

To the left when you step inside the apartment, there's a large room with a worn, herringbone wood floor. On one wall, an early twentieth-century cabinet: visible through its glass doors, a box of Clue, decks of cards, a couple of dictionaries, a ream of paper. Beside the cabinet, a metal rolling computer desk with shelves. A monitor on the top shelf; the desktop tower below. A sliding keyboard drawer.

Otherwise, the room is nearly empty. Three armchairs in no particular arrangement, a small table against a wall and two folding chairs with stacks of books and T-shirts draped over the back.

Two windows, the view of a street, not much traffic.

The final room is right off this room, through a set of swinging doors. In the space of a few square meters, three single beds in a row, with skinny nightstands in between and three screen dividers. After these three beds, that's it. A window faces a silent street.

The Home of the Mattress is on the mezzanine floor of a small Art Nouveau building. The furniture is vintage, somewhat decadent, frayed, and neglected, but not tacky. In the lobby, a large damp stain hovers like a cloud.

A short distance from here is Porta Susa, Turin's second station—for train inflow. Early mornings, you can hear the lines sizzling, announcing a train. Sometimes with a whistle for the go-ahead.

At night, the freight cars shift sleeping bodies in their beds. The whole district rolls over, swallows, coughs in the dark, goes back to sleep.

In that apartment, I has a mattress waiting for him. They pull it out from behind the cabinet whenever it's needed. The mattress is old and yellow but well-made: it's stuffed with raw wool, has vertical stripes, was probably soft in the beginning.

At least once a week, averaging twice a week, after his classes have finished, I sleeps at his friends'. Instead of walking through the historic center, reaching the station, boarding a regional train and traveling two hours outside of Turin, he'll take the tram to here.

There's a small neighborhood grocery store close by, where he'll stop first and buy some bags of frozen food with pictures of French fries on them, or shrimp, or precooked paella. He'll get cheap wine but always in the bottle; then he'll set off with his backpack and bag of groceries for the Home of the Mattress, and he'll push the buzzer under the three names written in pen.

Then it's the Formica table, the technical proof of independence, the staging of the end of adolescence. After dinner, it's someone's turn to wash the dishes, a few always left for the following day; then they sit and finish off the wine in their glasses, heads back against the wall, eyes closed. Except for one roommate, who's already gotten up halfway through dinner to go back to the computer. They don't talk much, never have a group discussion: they're either silent or suddenly all talking at once. No one talks about revolution; the important thing is not going back home to their parents.

I spends the night on the mattress, on the floor of the large room. His backboard is the cabinet and his nightstand is the floor. Before going to sleep he lays his book and glasses on the parquet floor beside him, then settles into his pillow. Always the same covers, same pillowcase, same sheets: never washed.

Beside him is Digital Guy, at one with the rolling computer desk. The flickering of the videogame spills over the mattress, flashes of color playing over I's silhouette, under the covers: every victory, every loss on the screen falls on him, bombs, explosions, tanks.

But all silent—at night, Digital Guy wears giant headphones. I only hears the chair squeaking with the twitching of the body seated above him, the tension of his attacks. Sometimes, he jerks, arches his back against the chair, which creaks and groans, like it might crack.

Sometimes the room swells with headlights off the street. Then the car leaves the scene, and the room goes back to its digital glowing war.

I stays awake a long while, staring at the floor, until four in the morning sometimes. No one ever sweeps in there. I gently blows on the floor, raising dust bunnies, planets slowly orbiting around him. They're light, form improvised constellations. Lying on the mattress, I disappears into this space, his own galaxy, a firmament of dust mites, sideral filth.

Then sleep comes, streaked through with panting from above, muttered swearing, elation, a slackening in contraction, the release of a chair orgasm.

The last thing I hears is Digital Guy getting up, usually toward dawn. He pushes the chair back in place. Then he steps over I and his mattress, like they're fallen space debris. He goes into the bathroom, the click of the light switch, flushing, then after, running water and a scraping toothbrush. Finally, the bedroom door is pushed open and a thud comes from the third bed.

In the large room, planets swirl over the one still there.

18

Prisoner's Home, 1982

It's on the second floor of a small building dating from the late 1960s. Rome reaches to here, then stops. Then there's what's left, kilometers of open fields, some just grass but also stretches of wheat.

The fields go on as far as you can see: an ocean of them; Rome is an island in the middle: the exception.

Prisoner's Home is in Apartment 1, though for four years now, Prisoner's been under marble, fifty kilometers from Rome, the inscription facing away from the Tiber that flows below, leading slowly back to Rome.

You take a few stairs to get to his place from the lobby. If you take the elevator, you'll see the door right when the elevator opens. There's a plain doormat, pretty much like all the others.

There's a last name by the doorbell; the name appears twice downstairs by the intercom buzzers, on the second and then the top floor.

The entryway includes a niche, and inside this stands a heavy piece of furniture, about waist high, with two terracotta figurines on top, a man and a woman, dressed from different periods, and underneath these statuettes are two doilies to protect the cherry wood. On the wall: a framed floral print.

The layout here doesn't really matter: it's similar to the other apartments above it, identical floorplan but increasingly bright.

What matters is the bedroom that's almost entirely filled by a queen-size bed with a laminated-wood frame and a thirty-centimeter gap between the mattress and the headboard and footboard.

Every night, a lady lies down on this bed: the grandma of the two children who live on the building's top floor.

The children come down to visit her every afternoon; if they're alone, they take the stairs; if their parents come, too, they take the elevator. They wait for the elevator doors to open, then ring her bell.

Afterwards, they run around the apartment, hide behind the doors, play hide-and-seek; they look for the perfect hiding place that no one can find. But they hope to be found—otherwise, it's no fun. The grandma pretends to search for them, calls their names in a loud voice. Then she hunts them down—they're usually lying pressed beneath the bed with their eyes squeezed shut.

Some nights they ask if they can sleep over; usually, they can; other times she sends them back up to the sixth floor.

In Prisoner's Home, the children each have a pair of pajamas, a few other things—socks, underwear, undershirts—and they always have toothbrushes in the bathroom.

If they sleep over, first they take a bath and then afterward, still red from the heat, they leap barefoot onto the bed. They sleep on either side of their grandma, under the blankets, like an angel with two wings.

When they've fallen asleep, the wings flap disjointedly; the angel rises in lopsided flight into the story's dark sky.

In front of the bed, on the floor, where a plasterboard wall once marked the true beginning of Prisoner's Home, there's now a dark stripe on the parquet wood. It's less than two meters from the back wall of the room, sealing off a rectangle of about four square meters. In theater, this would be enough to suggest a room. You'd see Prisoner locked up inside, even though Prisoner hasn't been there for four years.

And she doesn't know—and neither do her grandchildren—that he was there.

While the angel rises in lopsided flight into the story's dark sky, Prisoner sits on a bed and writes something down on a sheet of paper.

In the dark, through the puffs of night buses, you can hear the flapping of wings.

19

Relatives' Home, 1982

IT'S THE SAME TABLE FROM when Father brought Grandma to meet Relatives for the first time. Back then, I didn't exist and Sister was only three stomach spasms for Mother. By the third, a spray of vomit and wide-eyed, she knew she was pregnant. So a few days of agreed-upon silence and the visit with Grandma to Relatives' Home.

The entire time, Relatives looked at Grandma to try to understand who Father was. In her elegant, somewhat revealing, floral yellow dress, Grandma was a social enigma: immodest, lipstick somewhere between satisfaction and perdition, painted fingernails and toenails, and a flash of thigh through the slit in her dress. A cigarette, always.

And her glass always in reach and filled without the least encouragement from Relatives, and at every sip, her statements drenched in exalted despair. But showing a clear confidence as well, the confidence of a person from a solid background, with impeccable, inherited manners; and her alcoholic perspiration fused with the cloying scent of dead flowers.

The exact opposite, then, of Relatives. Them: a modest background but striving for a programmed existence, meaning, for boredom as a guarantor of a successful life, with no impulse to improvise, and no unforeseen twists of fate. The husbands with a bit of a paunch, TV on during meals. A respectable son-in-law was what they needed to be in the black.

So Relatives had first looked at Grandma, and then Father, heir to a shipwreck, spoiled by genetics, argumentative by nature and aware of his decline, the son of a fallen diva. And now the next son-in-law, an acquired relative through the careless daughter sitting next to him, already sadly impregnated.

When Sister arrived, then I, the first attempts at annexation began. Relatives have always invited Sister and I into their dining-room/living-room combo, offered them their TV, celebrated the rite of kinship around that same table. Father has always resisted. He loathes being alone with his failure, wants his entire nuclear family to sink along with him.

This time, annexation is a Polaroid. In the photo, I is on the balcony of Relatives' Home. All around, a display of sheets, and the communal polyphony of summer: children, dishes, untuned televisions, and the airy silence of the post-meal hour.

I is standing on the balcony in his soccer cleats and his red-and-yellow Rome uniform. He's posing for Relatives' photo, and his smile is frightened, because he knows Father considers this high treason. Relatives with their finger on the shutter button are his firing squad: the opening and closing of the shutter are the muzzle to the rifle. Load, then fire. At the very least, he should turn his back to them, let them get their shot in with him running away. But he gives them an embarrassed smile instead.

Father watches from the table; he's the only one who never gets up.

Then they're in the car, their plates still sitting on the table in Relatives' Home. Father grabbed I by the arm and yanked him off the balcony and the rest was shouting at the united block of Relatives. "I am so fucking sick of your shit," is the line I remembers.

Now Father's driving and he doesn't speak; the only thing that's clear: they're headed for the mountain. The highway is the certainty that for hours, there'll be no more getting out.

I is condemned to drive through Italy in his Rome Soccer uniform and cleats. Everybody has to see him sitting there in the back seat, says Father, that's what he gets—put in the stocks—dressed like a doofus on the A1.

20

Family's Elegant Home, 2011

THE FAMILY'S NEW HOME/ELEGANT VERSION, isn't that far from the first version, but it's far enough to make a difference. Just two streets over, but that's a number of rungs up the social ladder: from comfortable working class to well-entrenched upper-middle class. Wife, Little Girl, and I are still the same, but now they have a single last name over their doorbell, and in brass. It's I's last name, promoted to patriarch, or better, to the representative of a tradition that otherwise doesn't apply to a family put together with lonely, discarded pieces. Besides, I doesn't really believe in it—this tradition—and maybe Wife doesn't either, but they both like it, find it reassuring, infusing this project of theirs with a little practical motivation.

The size of the place is in keeping with its purpose: one hundred and fifty square meters, two bathrooms, marble floors, and where there isn't marble, there's parquet wood, like God commands. For Wife, this is a return to the class she left; for I, this is the realization of a middle-class dream. Rooms they have in abundance: five or six; plus the hallway lined with bookshelves—a place you can live in. Little Girl has her own personal realm; they call it her "little room," to add a childish note, but it's the size of a studio apartment. The most impressive of all is the corner room: five windows, an exemplary space, spreading its essence over everything set inside. Even I's nondescript couch, in this context, takes on an aura of torn luxury. The view out the windows: hills.

Outside, everything's just as elegant; the neighborhood is monochrome. Meaning, a circumscribed number of families passing bricks along on the hereditary axis. The urban planning here tends toward Art Nouveau. The buildings' balconies have decorative floral balustrades.

The other buildings here are small stores. Washed fruit is on display because the vegetable kingdom indicates good breeding. Prices are rarely marked, as this is vulgar. They're high, but that's reassuring: price determines clientele.

The neighborhood isn't generally philanthropic, though this doesn't exclude the occasional sentimental coin: it brightens one's mood, cements class spirit, and is mixed with the mortar of Catholicism turned ruling class, with some emotion added in, and just a pinch of environmentalism. At the grocery store exit, change and receipt are often dropped into the open palm of the Third World sitting against the wall. And along with this, the adjective "Dear" adds a sprinkling of paternalism. Because this is a personalized handout. Skin color and poverty aren't sufficient. An already established relationship is required. Continuity is fundamental here, the recognition that the outstretched hand is begging, not demanding, with a display of proper etiquette.

—

When they enter their new building, Wife, Little Girl, and I are greeted by a floor mosaic that reads: 1878. A show of heritage rather than resilience, of lineage even in brick. The building manager maintains it, cleans it twice a day. She's steeped in passive gentility by proximity—she's ferocious with delivery people and calls the condo owners "Sir" and "Ma'am," no matter their age. She addresses workmen in the same manner, but with an entirely different meaning. An expression of contempt, a cleansing politeness.

Class struggle—clearly, from her behavior—is a practice to be carried out no matter what: with those classes available to her in the building, she's chosen to fight her own whenever she sees it step into the lobby.

One look from her is enough to reveal that I's class standing is fake, a genteel backdrop in a papier-mâché theater. Because I is the only renter in the building, with a cosigned lease and a three-month damage deposit. This is evidence of a crisis for the building—an infiltration beyond the three founding families—but a moth-eaten, money-draining, empty apartment does more damage than a renter with a fixed three-year/two-year renewal contract and a flat-rate tax. If the financial crisis passes, they can give him the boot in five years and return to their former glory. If it doesn't pass, I can look after the place, keep the mites and insects at bay, and staunch the hemorrhage of expenses.

And if her looks aren't enough, the building manager also reminds him of his status at the end of the first month. She calls to him, adding "Sir," when he and Wife and Little Girl are almost out the front door. "May I remind you—I apologize for the intrusion—but your rent is coming due, the notary's asking for it." And she hands him a piece of paper, a memorandum from the notary, with an alphanumeric code and the last name of the owner. Then she slips back behind the glass door by the staircase. The curtain is drawn: she's off duty. Above this door, on a shelf, sits a Madonna and Child statue, which she also keeps clean.

21

Home of Savings, 2000

THE HOME OF SAVINGS IS a bank account. So it has the potential for size, can be cramped or expand indefinitely, across national borders. It has no land registration, doesn't touch the ground, has no foundation; it has a signature on a mutually binding contract, for the benefit of the bank that prepared it, as is common practice.

It's less a home than a barracks. Where I quarters his army, his small amount of money, considering he's twenty-five. I recruits resources for a more effective regiment. There's no great ritual to it—just the usual signature at the bottom of a document and another useless piece of paper to hold onto. With this, I assumes full responsibility for all those brought into the Home of Savings, with access to the mystery of cash flow.

No training required. Money is born trained: it enters already knowing how to handle a rifle, how to clean it, load it, release the safety, aim, the amount of resistance on the trigger. And of course it knows the rudiments of discipline, that you have to be tough to be in the military, you have to toe the line, follow orders, fight.

The truth is, it's Father who built the Home of Savings, when I was still a teenager. Walking from the Home Beneath the Mountain to the branch office, two bodies, two oblique, parallel shadows, I's obligatory comb, his shined shoes, Father barely saying a word as they walked. And in the end, I, embarrassed, sweaty hands in his pockets, standing in front of the windows to the bank, then in the lobby. And then the next humiliation, standing in front of the bank manager, such a sweaty palm, the skin secretions in front of this intermediary between I and money.

The bank assisted with the construction of the Home of Savings due to I's young age. With the rider, however, that Father stand guard in the barracks, as a guarantor. So: Father in the tower, eyes peeled, monitoring entrances and exits, criminal liability. All this with the approval of the branch manager and one final hand-shake—with Father—for having turned his son over. As a reward, the bank offered Father lowered banking fees and two-year—even three-year—personal planners for Christmas that could also be used for school. "From this day forward, Sir," the manager told I in farewell and investiture, "you represent this bank." This "Sir," this sense of regard, was I's first asset due to capital.

The walk back to the Home Beneath the Mountain was a silence in reverse, with Father proud and chatting up a storm, and I walking along with his hands in his pockets, quiet and in debt.

The laying of the first stone, then, was actually an invasion. Father supplied the initial squad: a patrol of his own money, as I didn't have any yet. The money clicked its heels, then invaded: a small force but still a permanent occupation. They settled into this empty space at once.

Father said, "It took forever to get this." Losing even one soldier would be another betrayal. Any casualty, any dollar casually spent, and there'd be blood to pay. So it was very clear: man the walls, polish your gun barrel, prepare to fire, budget for any collateral damage, wasted resources, innocent victims. Never, ever lose a single soldier. And that's how I was initiated into the art of war.

The Home of Savings has been growing ever since. Still no losses, so I can consider himself satisfied. And Father's still on sentry duty, even if he's no longer officially present. He's abandoned his post but left his eyes there, watching, bodiless.

I often inspects his troops. Takes a general look but also tallies precise units. He likes to sit and watch the parade, hear the jingle-jangle of coins going by. He finds this gratifying and also somehow shameful.

And he also worries quite a bit when he watches his squads depart. He checks their shoes, their gaze, posture, conviction; from the tower, those eyes, of course, control the controller. Then I sees them go, sees the door opening, and that's when his terror begins, his labored breathing that accompanies them as he stands there. He glances back at the rest of his troops, at how little money remains. For days it's all he thinks about. About when they'll return. At night he dreams of carnage.

22

Home of Poet's Death, 2018

THERE'S NO POINT TO LOOKING for the water: you can't see it from in here. You can hear it, maybe, but only for a couple of hours late at night, when there's a force 2 breeze, so around 4 knots.

During the day, all you can hear are tires on the road. And not that many—not much traffic on Via dell'Idroscalo. But the echo of every car lingers, tarnishes the air, and the light over the shacks makes a sound.

Mostly: the incongruity of it all, the rust, the trash in the road, the potholes, junked cars—a landscape of metal wreckage—all this erases the sea, denies it even as a hypothesis, a wandering thought.

Excludes any water at all, really, except in the potholes when it rains, and these puddles don't reflect the sky.

At night, when darkness takes over, when rust devours gates and car bodies alike, when the sea seeps secretly past the hedge, in the Home of Poet's Death, there's a dragging through the grass.

In fits and starts, usually less than a meter, then a pause, a slow crunching, clearly, of working jaws. Then another movement forward, another stop. A turtle, an ancient turtle by the look of her. The gatekeeper of the Home.

She works especially along the edges, traces the perimeter with her chewing. Along the gated entrance, dividing this place from the road, the sea, access to a cement escape route. The turtle attempts her escape in a ruminative manner: a removal of grass and a risky crossing of Via dell'Idroscalo.

What you hear in the night then is the slow chewing of grass and then the turtle's shell striking the bars, a percussion, a knock, then a weak, imperceptible vibration. A stubborn rhythm: every tap, the illusion of escaping her prison, the sound afterward testifying to her failure.

A matter of millimeters, really: the turtle manages to slip through, but barely. She's almost out, the bars are behind her, the grass she eats is on the roadside. If we were only heads, then she'd be free. Her eye suggests this: the suspicion of freedom, the eye widening, pure exaltation.

But her head is only the outpost, faulty synecdoche: the part for the whole doesn't always work. The neck's maximum extension, in this case, is four ample centimeters, the length of her escape. Then comes her carapace, the thump in the night against metal. The humming of the bars is a searchlight on the surprised fugitive in her first meter on the lam.

Her carapace is her incarcerator; what protects her condemns her.

When she's almost made it out, experienced the world outside, seen car tires up close, every time, the turtle turns back. A permanent percussion never leading to despair. If the turtle does give up, hours later, it's only because she's tired.

She stops her grazing, looks for the hole a few meters from the entrance, settles there. It's a pit, technical evidence of a graveyard.

And that's how it goes this night as well, on Via dell'Idroscalo.

Now the turtle slips into her quarters, cleanly, precisely. Then silence, just the wind whistling through the bars.

In the dark, beyond the gate, Poet's Death remains. The garden, all around, is a black lake. The glimmering moon is gagged by clumped clouds, cut off, detached from a blue backdrop, the black coming on, of the night.

Poet's Death is a cement tree, rising toward the sea. A compact tree, a monument, a mausoleum for a petrified century.

I has tried numerous times to see it up close, but can't get past the gate. He's done this instinctively, as if called to this, driving to the coast. Parking nearby, then staring at the tree through the bars. He hasn't heard the slow scratching of the turtle in the grass; every time, he's turned back. And here he is again before the gate.

Poet's Death has no leaves, is solid concrete, withstands the seasons, has rigor mortis from water, sand, and stone, and a guarantor of iron.

Where men die cement trees rise: the ground takes their bodies and gives back concrete. And so the cement tree grows upright, unaided, unwatered. The rain cleans it but provides no sustenance; the wind can't shake, can't bend it, only smooths it through the passing years.

Over the cement tree's foliage, a spider has spun her web. The slow weaving of a perfect geometric pattern, a spreading trap. The wind runs through the web but can't tear it away.

The spider clings to Poet's Death, a febrile resident, a relentless conjurer, lethal to her prey. Perhaps the spider's the only one to hear the sea or intercept it.

She's asleep now, in her hammock, just as the turtle sleeps in her pit. The gatekeepers of Poet's Death.

A car coughs, and I drives away.

23

Home of Stones, 1984

THE TENTH FLOOR: THE WINDOW, along the entire wall, frames the mountain. It's summer, but there's still snow on top, a reminder of winter.

The Home of Stones is a hospital, twenty-five kilometers from the Home Beneath the Mountain. Specifically, narrowing in, it's a room with four metal-framed beds, mattresses one meter off the white-tile floor. Beds all the same: two facing pairs, nightstand next to each. Headboard, footboard, also metal, seven vertical bars.

On the nightstands, books, glasses, magazines, flowers in full bloom.

The door to the room is almost always open. They can see out to the hall, Mother, especially, from her bed by the window. The slow, continual traffic, even at night.

A walkway mainly, shapes going by, white coats flapping, gurneys being pushed, rolling IV stands. A steady, unexcited, clattering stream. White shoes, coughing, squeaking wheels, the hum of voices. A polyphonic sloshing.

The door closes a few times a day. Doctors and nurses come in, pull the covers down to see the bodies. They examine the faces of the people lying in the beds. Leaning over, they look at them from the outside and from the patients' words, they ask what's happening on the inside, but sometimes their own words are merely tired.

Two of the four beds are occupied. One with a girl, or maybe she's older; she might be thirteen, might be twenty, might be sixteen. A lady is sleeping in a chair beside her bed. Probably her mom, since they look alike; the girl, head on her pillow, stares at the sleeping woman.

On the opposite wall, Mother lies in her bed. Hard to tell if she's asleep; she's not moving, anyway. On the floor, by the bed, her slippers, side by side. Awaiting her feet. Every now and then, Mother complies, slips her feet inside, and walks. Sometimes to the bathroom, just out in the hall. Sometimes closer to the window, to look out: at the windows of the houses, the tile roofs, the terraces and flowers, and in the distance, the stadium floodlights, the curving arena, the stands; and of course the gas station, the railway slipping off toward the mountains.

The Home of Stones is a parallelepiped on end.

A narrow building: if there's a strong wind, you can practically see it swaying when you look up from below. It sways along with the trees in the large, nearby park. The light from the windows swaying, bending, onto the surrounding rooftops while the patients in their beds moan their separate moans.

On Mother's nightstand, there's a small, clear cylindrical container, with a brown plastic cap.

A prize after her surgery; the same container the girl—or teenager—has on the other side of the room.

She—the girl—presents it like a trophy to her friends who visit. "Look what I had inside me," she says to all of them in the same voice. She holds up the container with the small stones, but almost no one takes it.

She laughs. "They won't hurt you. They're gallstones."

But Mother doesn't say anything when Father brings Sister and I during evening visiting hours. And she doesn't show them her prize.

Father doesn't say anything either. Those stones, in the plastic container sitting on the nightstand, are a defeat. Mother didn't dissolve Relatives entirely in acid—there they are. She didn't carry out her duty.

But Sister and I are happy to see her feeling better; maybe that means they won't hear her crying anymore in the middle of the night.

I walks over to the window, then looks back at the girl—or teenager—in the other bed, but doesn't have the courage to ask her what her name is; or to ask the woman who resembles her, in the chair beside her.

Then he goes back to Mother's bed, where Sister asks what that plastic container is with the pebbles inside. Mother smiles and says something no one remembers; she doesn't mention that it's a family photo.

24

Home of Adultery, 1994

THE HOME OF ADULTERY IS a single room, though it's not a studio apartment. Information isn't available about the apartment's overall size and floor plan. I's never had access to the entire place; the door's always remained closed.

The marble floor in the entryway is all that runs from this room to the rest of the apartment. The floor doesn't give a damn if the door's open or closed; it just slips beneath, undisturbed. And it has nothing to say; besides, every week, any trace of what it knows is washed away.

I is interested in that room. That's where the words form that Woman with the Wedding Ring says out the window. It's the incubator of language, the cave where the alphabet is worked over with saliva.

Whenever I steps inside, they have sex on the rug or on the couch. There's never time to undress, I with his jeans around his ankles, his pelvis driving him. Knees rubbed raw and bloody by the coarse rug.

—

It would be wrong though to say the rest of the apartment doesn't exist. Behind that door, in fact, is the Twins' realm, the habitat where they survive when their mother's stretched out on the rug.

Sometimes I hears them laughing, racing around. There are so many steps and all so quick, the apartment seems endless, circular. For quite a while, before he saw them from a distance, identical as they were, the only thing I knew about Twins was their footsteps: beyond the door to that room, Woman with the Wedding Ring was the mother of four rambunctious feet and a single laugh.

Sometimes I heard a thump, then came the double sniffles, then the wailing. But Woman with the Wedding Ring would already be on the other side of the door, and then the crying grew softer with her voice, and then it disappeared. Afterwards, the TV went on, and Twins became a background of recorded voices. Their presence became the TV schedule.

Today, Twins can reach the doorknob. They grew overnight—a centimeter in their sleep. They stood and for the first time, grasped the doorknob. And so Twins opened the door while I was with their mommy. The pair's first impulse: to freeze at that intimacy, stay quiet in that landscape of abandoned bodies.

Saying more would just be tattling.

25

Home of the Tumor, 2007

For I, the heart of the matter isn't so much the building as that room. It's that room he's jealous of, because he only knows the door, not what's behind it. I has Wife's words, sure, but they're not enough to *see*.

The building does have its importance.

An unnoticeable building surrounded by others in the dark. Hectares of darkness, a sort of lake encircled by a provincial road.

The building is at the center of this, an island of lit-up cement.

A military structure. Its guiding principles: compactness and isolation. Probably modeled after the Pentagon, both places for nuclear warfare. And here, every day, the attack is launched on the tumor's organized forces: rivers of money spent to destroy the cellular enemy, an extreme attempt at survival of the species. An outpost of constant activity; its specialty: chemical warfare.

But outside, you can't hear a thing. A silent conflict, echoless. All around, the night, the silent Alps, the stillness of the Cenozoic era, the crickets and cicadas and their loud chirping. The deserted parking lot, senseless rectangle perimeters in white, geometry of emptiness.

Fluorescent light spills from the windows and floods the surrounding area, about ten meters out from the building block; it devours the dark, discovers the fields, reveals what little there is, basically, blades of grass.

To get to the room, there's a series of hallways and closed doors. Not a labyrinth: above the exit a red light glows that's always on and can lead you outside quickly if necessary. A simplified labyrinth, then.

The doors are all the same, and white—it's white everywhere. White walls, white ceiling. The only black: the black protrusions of the doorknobs. This white color is eternal, not deriving from, not leading elsewhere. It's suspension, metaphysical resistance to the tumor, to its metastasis.

The hallways have no windows. But there are openings of sorts that aren't so different from real windows, with the various-sized frames hanging on the walls. These are, in their way, panoramas, the only concession to the sick.

They're posters of bank checks—the generosity on display of wealthy donors, publicly traded companies, local philanthropists, wine and paint manufacturers—amounts included, names in capital letters beneath. Signed and dated at the bottom, evidence of the donors' personal involvement, far different from a simple bank transaction. Yet at the same time, this is liquidity, a blood cleansing, goodness pumped through the financial vascular system. And so, intrinsically beneficial to the entire West, analgesic therapy, providing instant relief though with no permanent effect.

The hallways have these artificial openings at regular intervals. Windows with a capital view, corporate-generosity landscapes. Openings so the space feels less cramped, so you can breathe. Meant to be reassuring: to say we're in good hands, that war is war but look at all that heart.

The room is the barycenter.

A door mainly. Nothing special, white like everything else, invisible against the wall; you only see it when you have to step inside.

An otherworldly crossing, a passage to what comes after. To recover life, you must negotiate with death, play on its field. The door is an accessway. Leading to customs, admittance or rejection.

Wife knows what's behind that door; every week, for months, she trampled the grass of passing. A short negotiation but with several stopovers. Death doesn't just give up what's rightfully hers, she'll blow up the bargaining table, raise her demands, issue ultimatums.

After every session, Wife returned among the living. She carried death with her, visible on her flesh, her fingernails. She displayed the consequences of these negotiations at the dinner table, carried them around on her bike, at the movies, at the grocery store, while sitting at a restaurant.

So she went back behind that door and continued to negotiate.

All this happened before I knew her.

Sometimes Wife went in there to negotiate with death while her father was with her, or a friend, or her sister. They know what's on the other side. They sat at the table, played lawyer. Not I. They know how to describe the color of death's eyes, the shape of death's hand, if there are freckles on death's face. Not I.

They're the ones who brought her back out, returned her to the living.

I only has that scar to look at, on her breastbone. He's staring at it now, while Wife sleeps, leaning over her in the room's dim light.

MODULARIO
F. rig. rend. 497

MINISTERO DELLE FINANZE
DIPARTIMENTO DEL TERRITORIO
CATASTO EDILIZIO URBANO (RDL 13-4-1939, n. 652)

MOD. 3N (CEU)

LIRE 500

Planimetria di u.i.u. in Comune di ■■■ .... via ■■■ .... civ. ■■ ......

piano ■■

B.B - 0402107

h mt 2.70

Scala 1:1000

ORIENTAMENTO

SCALA DI 1:200

26

Family's Elegant Home, 2011

(And then there's the voice of the apartment when everything is quiet, the nighttime voice of Family's Elegant Home, when the three bodies living there don't really matter, when they occupy far less space than the furniture. It's a conversation between separate species, between wardrobes, nightstands, and kitchen tables, between moths, the electric hum of the fridge, and the click of wood settling, announcing that even without roots, the wood is no less alive. A muted conversation, not anticipating human ears— sometimes I turns his head, and everything grows still, only an echo remains, the last woodworm chews a bit distractedly, then goes silent, rejoining the mass, the rest of the secret, and I falls back to sleep. But by some remote chance, if the sound continued and could be heard, the conversation would be different from that of the first Family's Home, even if the furniture's the same. Here, there's not the same self-importance from Wife and Little Girl's linen chest— inherited, a symbol of belonging and therefore of acquired senior-ity—while it speaks with I's blue wardrobe that stands beside it; and the bookcases and chairs stretch out across the room from each other; and I's couch and Wife's walnut desk share the same space now, neither staking any particular claim. In short, there's no longer that sense of reluctance, of taking sides, of the long face even an armchair can pull. That, in the end, they might not make up a family—if you can ask that of furniture—but nighttime Elegant Home is a forest where everything happens together, where a click is answered by a creak, and Wife sleeps, and I sleeps beside her, and Little Girl shifts to get comfortable on her pillow, with the hills beyond, and the city's street lamps below, along the avenue.)

27

Home Beneath the Mountain, 1985

THE TRAIN STATION IS A stationmaster's house at the edge of town.

A classic color, Pompeian red, modest-sized. Two stories: the main floor for passengers, and above this, the stationmaster's quarters.

It's been a layover station for a while now, with a web of tracks. For a century it was ready for numerous trains, with a full complement of the proper equipment, which the stationmaster operated by a manual switch. Not that much work for him, not much impact on his day: heading downstairs, clearing the traffic, diverting trains to other lines. Not a large concentration of trains, but with important symbolic value, in the town's secular marking of time.

Though not bronze like the church's bell, the station did have its smaller version: cheaper, an alloy of tin and copper, mainly tin, for the tone. A small knocker compulsively, almost hysterically, tapping on the bell.

The stationmaster's house was a kind of rectory. No real mystery to the first floor: open windows, clattering plates, laughing children. The family's laundry, a score of colors, shirt sleeves, and trousers on the line. The real destination of those arriving by train, the town flag, smelling of detergent and fabric softener.

At night everything was quiet, the freight train came through at night and didn't stop, just headed toward its destination. The stationmaster would watch it pass from his window. The freight train disappeared around the curve, always with the same rumble, the same displacement of air from its great weight. Then the stationmaster would toss out his cigarette butt, close the shutters, and the day was done.

All this happened in the past, is I's mythology, memory turned to art, the words of others, things he's heard, sepia-toned photos, all spun into I's memories.

Before I ever lived in the Home Beneath the Mountain, the station had been downgraded to an unmanned stop. These were the early trials of production engineering, management control, expense optimization. Which meant the first floor of the stationmaster's house was now permanently closed; the stationmaster had been moved to an office, his hat tucked in a closet; and he slept in the more customary way, with his family, in a small building in town.

And now I is here, below the closed shutters of the stationmaster's house, with Grandma. A suitcase at his feet. He carried it through the entire town: being big is mainly a show of strength, an act of will. And it doesn't matter that the suitcase is almost as large as he is, with his scrawny, ten-year-old frame.

From the windows overlooking the road, from the soccer field, everyone saw Grandma and I walking across the town, one behind the other, in a procession. They all saw a boy and a lady walk a bit, then stop so the boy could set down the heavy object. They all saw

Grandma try to help, I pull away, holding her back with his hand, and then grabbing the suitcase by the handle and starting off again.

No talking, but everyone's breathing was anxious.

Grandma said, "Don't worry. Father feels very alone. It's not true he wants me dead—sometimes it's painful to him that he was born, and I'm the one who brought him into this world, so he takes it out on me. But he's not a bad man. He'd never hurt me, or any of you."

He only hurled her suitcase down the stairs and pushed her out the door. He said: "Go with her to the station—she's taking the first train." I, in his shorts, picked up her suitcase, while Grandma smoothed her dress and kept from screaming.

And then came the procession, the Via Crucis through the streets of town.

I can't say why, doesn't know what happened in the kitchen while he was gazing at the mountain, but now he knows it's only the problem of being born, the pain of entering the world. He knows his father is also a son.

Then there's the bell (remote-controlled now), and the approaching train. The repeated strikes against copper and tin, under the closed, first-floor shutters. Chanting the time of the things in this world.

Grandma says: "You've gotten so big, Honey."

Her voice is raised, competing with the train, the dark, halting shadow.

Then there's only a boy on the pavement.

I lifts his chin, peers through the glass.

Then walks away.

28

Red Home on Wheels, 1978

THIS IS THE LAST ADDITION of Prisoner's Home, the final addition. A Renault 4. Red. Six windows on four sides. From any point within, turning your head slightly, you can see the outside world.

That red—I recognizes that color. The glowing mouth of the TV injected it into his nervous system while he scuttled around the Underground Home. As a result, though he doesn't remember it, I feels that color like a twinge in his hip, a kind of national pain; he'll always remember that color, won't be able to distinguish it from blood.

In the entranceway there's a nameplate with the name: Rome N57686.

There's also a number, 90, in white on a round, red sticker. This is the speed, while traveling, that the Red Home must not surpass.

Now, however, the doors are closed. No one's inside, or so it seems. Early morning, other cars parked in front and behind it.

Alongside a church; three steps to climb, up to the portal, but the church is closed and no one would hear. The church has remained still for over a thousand years, while everything around it is in motion.

Prisoner's Last Home has been there a few hours, or a few minutes—the blink of an eye compared to the eternity within the church.

The church façade is squeezed behind a grid of tubes, wood scaffolding, steel ladders, rails, wall bolts. Even eternity needs repairs.

At the end of the street, behind the church, other cars go by, then disappear, in the direction of the Forum, headed toward 300 BC.

Not many, but they'll increase soon, blend to one multicolored, wheeled form.

The lights are all off in the Red Home.

Something's been done to the backseat.

In the trunk is a wool, camel-colored blanket that's wrapped around something substantial, filling the trunk, a half cubic meter.

The blanket covers Prisoner's lifeless body.

The corpse fills the space.

Prisoner is curled up like a fetus. Ready to come out, to pierce through to the outside world.

It's dark in there, with perhaps just the thinnest trickle of light.

Prisoner is well-dressed: a blue suit, striped shirt, tie knotted at the throat; a vest, maybe. Black shoes.

His hair is combed, head slightly raised. It lies outside the soft wall of blanket, on the spare tire. Near Prisoner, a plastic bin of snow chains.

By Prisoner's feet, under the blanket, a plastic bag. A bracelet and wristwatch inside. Prisoner's death endowment. His dead body has blocked time, while the watch, still ticking, has jumped ahead.

People have gathered. The street's blocked off; the church is still closed.

Two men in uniform open the trunk; they see the blanket, understand its bulky contents. Standing next to them, a priest.

In the open trunk, perhaps some sunlight falls on Prisoner. The light might flicker, might be still, hard to say.

The men lean over, pull back two corners of the blanket, expose the huddled body.

All the other faces peer in, but no one speaks. Then someone recognizes him and says his name, as if he's just been born; he says it really is Prisoner.

And so his death is born, and in a few hours, is in the paper.

The priest—on national television, I only a lowercase *i* among all the others in front of their TV sets—makes the sign of the cross over him.

29

Home Inside the Fence, 1995

THE TABLE COMES FROM THE Home Beneath the Mountain, the table crammed into the corner by the window. Now, at last, it has its very own room, can finally spread its wings: the era of humiliation is over, its two semicircles can break free, the leaf rising from its housing to keep them apart. The circle can now renounce its stagnant state of closure, can relax into an oval.

Like any piece of furniture, the table arranges people and is unconcerned with its surroundings; that the mountain's gone, replaced with some sort of cityscape, doesn't matter in the least, because it's snowing out there, it's Christmastime, and there's a game board sitting in the middle of the table. And around that cardboard magnet, Father, Mother, Sister, Grandma, and I all take turns rolling the dice and moving their pieces.

It's a worn-out ritual, the obligatory mise-en-scène of childhood and the family nest. But childhood's too splintered to be handled without getting hurt. The gameboard is spread on the tablecloth, after the meal: it's like a parade for a regime that no one believes in anymore: everyone in uniform, everyone unhappy, praying it will end. That Grandma's here, visiting the new Home for the holidays, certifies, legitimizes the scene. Sister and I, in their twenties, are locked into behaving like children, rejoicing on cue at the fall of the numbers, the dice establishing the proper emotional code.

On the gameboard, a stylized floor plan to a mansion: a search for the murderer, moving the murder weapon from room to room. A much larger home than the one where this game is taking place, but with the same element of blame: Father thinks it's Grandma, Sister and I are united against Father. Mother just hopes it won't end the way nearly everything always ends, that she can stay inside this fiction, keep it from breaking, keep from getting slapped.

But this time the tension's not so choking: I's the murderer, Mr. Green, the murder weapon is the candlestick, and the room is the library. I wants to protest, but stays quiet, and everything goes back in the box without drama. The Home Inside the Fence has been Christened, the ceremony has come to an end.

That afternoon, Father walked Grandma through the apartment, his pride ill-concealed, his annoyance showing. He'd driven her from the station to this reinforced concrete cube in the middle of the neighborhood; he somehow reproached her with this, his own solidity compared to her dissipated life. The flashing light on the fence let them in, a safe maneuver—almost a U-turn—to a reserved parking place. He helped her out of the car, taking her hand, carrying her suitcase up.

There are six cubes in all, fenced off and isolated from their elegant surroundings. Outside this enclosure is a provincial residential neighborhood—the city chasing the countryside away, scaring it off with bulldozers. Then planting grass plots in memory of farm fields, a geometric commemoration, tomb-like. An edger used throughout: details matter, determine the style. Geraniums on the balconies add a finishing touch.

The Home is the same as all the others inside the fence. An entryway, two bedrooms, living-room/dining-room combo plus kitchen, drywall interior, windowless bathroom: a rectangle, seventy square meters, divided into five decorous spaces and two balconies. The six cubes shape the complex registered to a state-owned company where Father works. The underlying idea here is that state identity is composed of concrete. It's everything alike in here, one big cement landscape.

But the real point is the dream of it: a fixed rent and the prospect of becoming a homeowner in a few years for an off-market amount. Basically, aspiring to "forever," but without the normal monthly cadence tied to salary and rent.

When Grandma finishes walking through the Home Inside the Fence, she says, "Very nice. I'm happy for you." But clearly she's not; this is the exact opposite of what she likes—but he's also lucked out—things could have gone much worse. "Very nice," she says again, "I'm happy for you," and this is the comment of a mother. "Picture it," Father says, "without all the boxes." Mother, Sister, and I stand off to the side, a few meters away: a separate family on stage at the moment, a scene from a couple of light years away, from a past they're not a part of.

In the kitchen, Father studies the boxes stacked against the wall, studies the ceiling, the baseboards. He says: "It's not very big, but it'll be forever." He doesn't mention that the State's "forever" differs from the eternal, that it's a type of forever offered to the non-wealthy, that is, ninety-nine years—and much more than any of those present, including I, can register. But it's the forever

Father can offer to his family: a concrete forever, with a contract and a countdown that's not scary just then. In a hundred years, none of them will be around to see the moment when, at the strike of the final second, the home will return to nothing, its soul slipping through the walls.

30

Home Over the Rooftops, 2004

PARIS IS EASY TO IMAGINE. It's already in our heads, so takes little effort. Firsthand knowledge isn't necessary. The stereotype, the frozen imagination, will do. All it takes is a little microwaving in the brain.

Put the verbal activators in, set to defrost. Punch in "Tour Eiffel," "Bateaux Mouches," "Seine," "Bouquinistes." Add "Montmartre" and "artists' square."

Now Paris is ready to serve. You can hear the voices, the accordions; see the vibrant purple lights; smell the crêpes.

Once the city's opened, try homing in. Focus on Montmartre; turn away from Sacré-Coeur, turn back, note the portrait painters in the square; set some tourists in the chairs. Head into the district; let the voices fade.

At the building on the corner, type in the entrance code, 8BC2.

Now step onto the elevator, and press 7.

Turn on the hall light; go to the last door on the right.

Imagine fifteen square meters, a perfect rectangle. Set I on a chair, elbows on the table, clearly a young man now. A window over the rooftops.

—

A shopping bag sits by the front door, a tower of cans, cheap beer, the offering I pays to the senselessness that's brought him here: basically, to escape, avoid paying rent, and at least console himself with the jealousy of others. The geography of his foolishness is European and passes through capitals: Berlin, Amsterdam, Paris. Homes he's been offered, out of a sort of scared orphan syndrome: he attracts patrons who have run out of time and just want to give someone else a little affection, and perhaps contribute to the possibility of future glory. Every time, I thanks them, packs his bags, then moves and retreats inside this new home.

He slips out of the apartment each week for those cans and for packages of frozen food. He walks down the hill, stands in line, pays, goes back to the apartment, and then slowly consumes these items, like Turtle with her lettuce behind the flowerpot. Sometimes on his return trip with his shopping bag, he cuts across the artists' square; he doesn't stop but does look at the painters painting those faces in such a painterly manner. He looks at them as if they're part of a calming, judicious panorama, where tourism is reason enough.

The Home Over the Rooftops is a box with three windows, including one with a balcony. A mansard, a one-room studio.

There's not much space, according to the deed: three by five meters. But there's an angel of illusions at work here—with beer doing its part—because I sees two rooms and a kitchen. More even: a kitchen, a bedroom, and the office, where he happens to be sitting.

A northwest exposure, in the direction of the Channel Tunnel and the Port of Le Havre.

The kitchen's on the left when you enter the apartment. Essentially, an electric portable cooktop sitting on a shelf. With two burners, meaning two round, cast-iron hotplates of two different sizes: the smaller burner, good for frying eggs and making coffee. The larger burner for everything else.

The small balcony, directly off the kitchen, resembles a forklift cage: standing room for one. I has tried to squeeze a chair out there, so he can sit and read and take in the view. The chair fits, but not a body and a book. So I goes out on the balcony and stands and reads.

The space I calls his "office" is actually circumscribed by a red rug with blue detailing. Technically, a faded tapestry. A small, cheap table sits on the tapestry, a modest wooden desk with an equally modest chair. On the table, a laptop (always on), an open notebook, a few books, a glass of water, some paper, Post-its, handwritten notes. The table sits in front of a window, the paper blind pulled down, blocking out Paris.

Inside this space, I spends many hours a day typing on his laptop. He enters early in the morning, crossing the threshold of the tapestry, and only exits for bodily needs.

This office is, in fact, a ring: to enter, he only needs to cross a fabric line. And in this ring, he punches the alphabet. He's always on the attack, never defends himself. He drops his chin, convinced that's all it takes to enter a sentence, to get it on the ropes. He doesn't do much dancing around—he's stubborn and always hits in the same spot, and when the alphabet hits back, he doesn't react, just stands stock-still and lets it strike.

At night he climbs out of the ring, leaves the tapestry, and retreats to the bed.

The "bedroom" is the third room of his Parisian studio apartment. If he exits the tapestry, it's another meter to the right. I rises from his chair and a few steps later is on the mattress. A queen-size bed, the bedding only rumpled on the right side, where I sleeps. In the morning, the left side is still smooth, sheets ironed, feather pillow still plumped, no creases. I wakes up, pulls back the covers, gets out of bed, pulls the covers up on his side. Then there's showering, heating the small pot of milk, breakfast on his feet and into the ring once more, fingers on the keys, the wheel turning the hands of the day. And while he writes, that question—what am I doing here?—is always set aside.

(Then there's Paris, the real Paris I slips into late at night, usually on the weekend. To survive, mainly, to save himself another way, and so he walks, exhausted, along the endless Seine, or among the hedges of the Tuileries Garden. Sometimes he winds up at a bar in Belleville or Bastille, and now and then in some unknown bed, a damned, nonresident poet—where everything almost always turns out badly, but when he wakes up there's a new place to see and consoling caresses—and in the morning he retreats to over the rooftops, inside the words, and double-locks his life, yet again, inside a final parenthesis.)

31

Poet's Last Home, 1962

It's Poet's Last Home: to be clear, the one he won't be returning to. But for now, this home's not even masonry. Through a deed, all necessary documents included, it occupies very little space, although countersigned by all involved parties. It's built, so to speak, on lined paper with normal margins, the left margin, two centimeters, twice that on the right.

It will be built when the negotiating's through. The deed, more than anything, is a promise to build.

The document, now on file, is the only legal authorization for the real-estate transfer: this paper is bureaucracy's true public ground, the foundation of the State. The rest is money interwoven with the alphabet. Language, pieced together with the mortar of money, is the building block of power. The Notary is evidence of this union, so his fee can never be too high.

The buyer, obviously, is Poet. We see his signature among the others on the protocol sheet: it's clear, almost crude, and commits to millions of lire in two separate deposits. And takes on a bank mortgage.

Poet's Last Home, rising on a lined protocol sheet on November

12, 1962, is a future building. A property, according to the deed, located in a suburb of Rome, an area not intended for the construction of elegant villas or private gardens—with no luxury features, in accordance with Law No. 408 of July 2, 1949.

The neighborhood where Poet's Last Home will be built—the EUR—is the monumental evidence of how much a show of failure, in Italy, is the very origin of power. Founded where Il Duce planted a phallic pine tree with a ceremonial, triumphant spade and designed to connect Rome to the Tyrrhenian Sea, its name is the acronym for "Esposizione Universale Romana," the World's Fair that never took place in Rome. A triumph of reinforced concrete and imperial rhetoric, and tons of nails, iron, and cement. The monumental symbol upon which a nation might be founded: the importance of articulating a promise as the beginning and the conclusion of a process, with no thought of what comes after. Taking for granted that all that matters of this promise is the meaning of the individual words.

The urban result is to inhabit this failure—in this case an event that never occurred—as if it were a triumph: to innervate this failure with streets—inject it with life, cars, stores, hospitals—and offer it up as an exemplary model. Everything converted, finally, to propaganda: the money, cooled down to concrete, has risen to the sky, in harmony and consensus; the rest hardly matters, and that promise is now just a scrap of paper.

The building still lacks a street number, but it's set on lot 105 of the EUR plan, parcel 52. Affixing a number 9 by the driveway breathes life into the deed. From now on it will forever be recorded in the cadastre, the land registry, by which the State decrees the annexation of space.

It's a garden-level apartment, facing west, apartment number 2; it has six rooms, a couple of bathrooms, a private courtyard, a light-well, a stairwell, an access ramp to apartment number 3 with private courtyard. Plus, a seventh space, a garage on the lower level.

But the space of Poet's Last Home still means nothing, is just a floor plan—attached to a deed—deprived of the connective grammar of the bodies that will dwell there.

In the presence of buyer and seller, Notary celebrates the liturgy of private property, transforms words to possession. And by bringing pen to paper, by signing his name, Poet wields his power, asserts himself in real estate, and throws down the gauntlet to his own death.

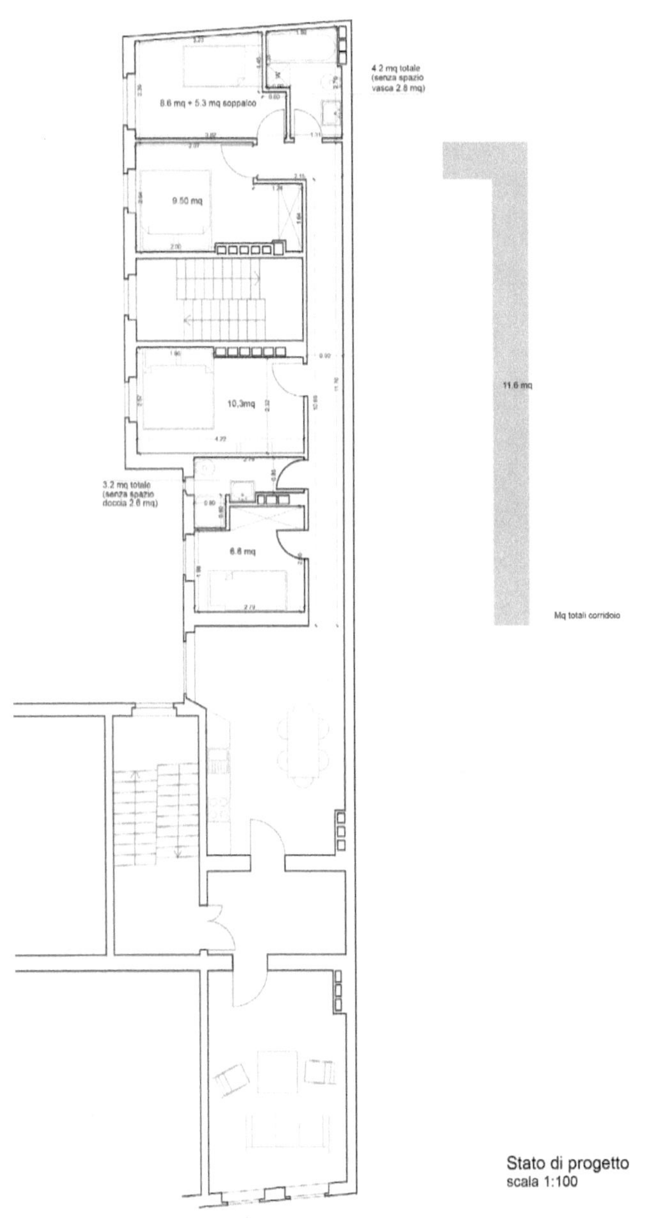

Stato di progetto
scala 1:100

32

Friendship Home, 1990

THE SPACE LIGHTS UP ONLY with the glow of an intermittent ember. Otherwise, it's cubic meters of darkness, sealed in by a main garage door. Actually, there's a ceiling grate, and the icy, dim light that filters through reveals the surrounding world: a concrete labyrinth, barred rectangles of light, and a series of individual garage doors, all alike. Each with a number to a corresponding apartment. What's unseen in an apartment building, what's been repressed, the emptiness it was built upon. A place outside the tyranny of the gaze: from here it will resurface, as surface, in a world designed, instead, to be observed.

In this case, what's above is a flower bed and then above this is the mountain. Plus the vertical stockpiling of families inside apartments, including, of course, the Home Beneath the Mountain, where I lives.

But the focus now is mainly that intermittent burning ember in the world below, in one of the garages, door raised. An ember that sometimes lights up a nose, and then a different nose and a pair of glasses—out-of-style glasses. I's glasses on I's nose; and behind the lenses, his eyes, when visible, are closed. The other eyes, above the other nose, are open: the ember briefly reveals exaltation, as the pupils retreat. Then darkness sets in again, saturates the space, leaving only the dim light from the grate to seep into the Citroën, the two boys inside, in the front seats, car doors open.

Above, it's night; the official story for each of them: taking out the trash, then going for a walk.

When one face lights up, words seep from the other's mouth. I keeps talking, endlessly; the other mainly throws out enthusiastic comments. They both talk about sex to avoid talking about love. Neither of them has much to say, so when the sex talk is over they talk about their fears. There's only time for one joint, so never more than ten minutes, usually a couple of invented sexual encounters and five or six fears. School's a subject in reserve and family never comes up; family stays put upstairs. The session always ends with the quality of the hash.

And the final act: lowering the garage door. And a red-eyed, resistant return to the world. They don't say goodbye, so no one else will hear. They disappear through two separate doors—each boy sucking on a mint—and step onto two separate elevators that extract them from the underground and return them to their families. What's left below is concrete, a buzzing of florescent lights, and the emptiness that props up the entire world. And the gift of that cloying scent the grate allows to seep into the unhappy apartments. Someone might just catch a whiff, nostrils flaring, lips playing briefly in an unconscious smile.

33

Home of the Newborn Furnishings, 2000

IN AND OF ITSELF, THIS home isn't all that important. Its obscurity is what sets it apart and erases it from any maps. And few traces of it remain for I, dispersed throughout his cerebral cortex. It's in the area where historical Turin fades to apartment buildings, to unremembered respectability, purgatorial urban planning sprinkled with green spaces and playgrounds.

A place facing the mountains, the tops lopped off by the windows of the second floor. The ringing of the church bell is clear, as is the clanging of the market booths—the backbone of neighborhood life—as they're put together. The day ends with them being taken down again, with smashed cardboard and rotten fruit in the street.

The Home is the square meters indicated on a contract, and not very many at that. A bedroom and kitchen, normal layout, both with a fair amount of space for moving around, though I seldom does. His inclination is to head to the city's historic center, to shut his door and head for the bus stop. So the Home is nearly always empty, left to the furnishings. As a result, I knows little about this neighborhood, except the street he takes to leave.

The furnishings, then, are the most important element, and

represent the execution of a mandate: the check Father handed him, a sum written on it, then spelled out, so I, with no vocation for marriage, could at least become a family of one. What's important—to be fair—is that Father wrote a check for the same amount to Sister when she married.

And so I has married his furnishings. Consistent with the mandate, he opted for a middle-class marriage and a lack of invention, of abdicating aesthetics and a personalized space. So on to the furniture factory, the most advertised furniture factory, near the freeway entrance for Milan.

He didn't have to do anything, just walk into his apartment, find it all assembled, and say he was satisfied. A kitchen designed along one wall—lacquered cherry, particleboard cabinets—a ventilated range, hood with two-speed fan, upper and lower wall units mirroring each other. The table in the same style, same finish as the cabinetry, with four chairs, though it can seat six. In the corner, a sofa bed, simple, tan. In the bedroom, a double mattress and bedframe, a desk, a wardrobe painted blue, divided into three sections, the middle section with frosted-glass doors and lights when these doors are opened.

And then the financial statement, the total coinciding with the exact amount on the check, everything accounted for, down to the last penny, and the final number rounded up.

Not much more to say about the place. The four-year fixed/four-year renewable contract signed at the agency is the direct result. Judging by the time I spends here, the term of the contract will probably be even less. When he's home, he relaxes as if he's in someone else's life, which might be reassuring if this was a life he wanted. It's not that he necessarily feels bad about the place, though, because what's the alternative? The wardrobe's half empty; all he uses in the kitchen is the oven. He has invited friends over, but that didn't have anything to do with the place's décor, and besides, he's stopped.

Probably, no memories of the Home will stay with him, but this is the place where I's furniture, one Tuesday in early fall, was born. It was here, on a sunny day of yellowing trees, that the furniture forced its presence, its volumes, onto I. And it was from this apartment that the furniture burst forth, to begin its endless wanderings in time and space.

Issuing from this place, the furniture will lay down the law forever: from now on, it will be the furniture that has the last word wherever I hopes to live, on the size of the place, the height of the ceilings, how the objects are arranged, the clothes, the pasta and other food items in canisters and tins. It will be the furniture, disassembled, reassembled, loaded, unloaded—by I or by movers—that will reject various options. The furniture will impose its tastes. From now on, everything will bear its likeness, and the tearing of a check will echo forever.

34

Home Beneath the Mountain, 1985

THE VIEW IS FROM THE walkway, the street view.

Basically, the street sees a window. Sees I in the window looking out, staring, behind the glass. Not much movement to see, including in those eyes. To say those eyes are asking for help would be a lie. There's no request here, no possible message to relay; just a basic condition.

Sometimes the street sees Father open the glass door and step onto the balcony. When this happens, I disappears. The Home Beneath the Mountain turns into a cube of silence: the silence of space, the death of the voice.

No child outside the family has ever set foot inside the Home Beneath the Mountain. While his classmates invited him over, expecting to be invited in return, I never invited them in return. Even if the requests came directly from their mothers, no little spy was able to report back on what happened beyond that closed window.

When the pressure became too great, when I could feel it, he instinctively stopped visiting the other boys' homes and went back to sealing himself inside that cube. And he left an empty spot inside his friends' playrooms.

So the street went back to guessing, envisioning that space and Father as a guard with no keys.

And then the street began to feel compassion, as it watched I with resignation, saw him at that window, and the nothing that the street knew was filled with sorrow.

And now we'll stop; anything more would be mawkish. Save that the compassion I felt from the street, reaching him through the glass, would be the bars to his prison.

35

Forever Home, 2010

THE FOREVER HOME IS CIRCULAR in structure, with the shape and nature of a wedding ring. One of the most technologically advanced of architectural finds: it can disappear inside a palm, can be tucked into a pocket. The exact size of the Forever Home, where I happily resides, is a circumference: 7.28 centimeters, to be exact, with a diameter of 2.37 millimeters. Empty, it weighs about 4 grams. With I inside, it's 4 grams plus 87 kilos.

It's built entirely of gold, so it's precious, dazzling. When the sun is high overhead, the Forever Home radiates light and is at its most defensible, this light, a dazzling screen which I can rest behind. No one will ever bother him behind this screen as no one's eyes can take in so much glare.

A few details on the interior. The floor and ceiling have the same curvature: there's no break in continuity between what's above and what's below. There's a single flow, space in eternal motion: every millimeter chases the millimeter before, with no intention of ever passing. The future is a fife player and every minute that's already passed parades behind it.

Floor and ceiling, if this distinction even makes sense, are smooth and unencumbered. On one section of the vault: some lettering and numbers. The letters form Wife's name, and the numbers are 5-30-2009. Gold removed from the surface of the Forever Home; the missing part is what you read.

Depending how the wheel turns, the engraving either sits on the top or on the bottom: sometimes Wife is the firmament; sometimes she's simply underfoot.

Aside from I, there's nothing inside the Home—he's the real furniture.

He entered on the date engraved on the vault, and he hasn't left since. He entered with his finger, his ring finger, and then made himself at home. But given the architectural nature of the place, of course he's moved: he's traveled the world, carrying the Home with him. He's put into practice what Turtle taught him long ago. Now that he resides in the Forever Home, he finally understands Turtle, how reassuring it is to always have a roof over your head. He walks around with his golden carapace, entirely fearless: almost his whole body can be outside his shell, stretching out, brushing up against all the things within his grasp. He does this with disbelief, barely aware he's doing it at all, though he does it with a kind of courage.

What he never would have dared before: he used to walk around naked, roofless, always ready to duck for cover. Now he walks defiantly, knowing he can recoil back inside whenever he wants.

This is enough for him to be able to step into the world, ready for battle, to brave bad weather, feel protected from rain, snow, the cold. It's enough, while he's walking or talking with someone, to touch the walls, run his fingers along the roof, to make sure the Home is still there.

And when he's tired, as he is now, on a plane headed for Berlin, when he feels all alone up in the sky, when the place where he'd like to be is locked up down below, sealed beneath a lid of clouds, when he feels the tears welling in his eyes though he can't allow himself to cry—when all this happens—I is grateful for his home. He thinks of Turtle and retreats inside his golden shell.

He lies down on the floor of his home, shuts his eyes and takes slow, deep breaths. Then he opens his eyes again and looks at the constellation of letters carved into the ceiling; his sigh spells out the name written there, which is part comfort, part pain. From that firmament on high, Wife looks down on him, protects him. And he reads the inscribed numbers, the date beside the name. He reads these numbers over and over, whispers them: they're the combination that opens the safe of his good mood. Then afterward comes sleep, his temple pressed against the window.

36

Home of Escaped Memories

The home of memories escaped from I's memory lies outside any real location: it's a crease in the space-time continuum. Hard to tell if it's still or in motion, if it's subject to the forces of Heaven or Earth.

The Home of Escaped Memories is the black box of what he doesn't remember, what his memory has refused, even if it happened. It's what allows I to steadily say I while knowing it's a lie.

Imagine a carnival attraction, a Plexiglas box with a mechanical arm and crab claw that attempts to clutch what's lying on the sandy bottom. Stuffed toys, watches, scuba masks. Consider a person's eagerness and zeal in manipulating that arm, grasping what he'd like, has always wanted.

Now see that triumphant sneer while that arm rises, the crab claw squeezing some object, then opening, dropping the prize into the winner's trough. And then consider the frustration at the rising arm, claw closed, nothing in its grasp, just some grains of sand the swinging mechanical arm chucks into the void.

For the sake of simplicity, think of I's mind as that box, his memories, the deposit of dolls and toys left on the sandy bottom. Imagine the mechanical claw clutching memories, and I who sees them briefly soaring overhead, then falling, hurtled into the sand, covered in sand once more.

Now concentrate on that sand and the objects buried there. A deposit invisible to I, which he tries to access from the outside, by maneuvering a lever. No matter his precision and his luck, the number of attempts, the many coins he slips into the slot, the mechanical arm and claw will never free his memories.

I doesn't know the world beneath the sand, how many objects, faces, facts are buried there. He knows this world exists, and that's the only thing he can tell himself for certain. He'd like to pound on the box, shake it to shift the sand.

But in spite of everything, I never stops trying. Because he knows, without really knowing, that she's inside the Home of Escaped Memories, that there, in among all that clutter of memories, is Sister. She's the queen of that sandy underground world. She's the one, within the silence of all those grains of sand, who sees the very tip of a claw widening a gap every day in what, for her, is a dark, dull sky, that disappears soon after.

This is where I has buried her, and is perhaps the reason he keeps flailing away at digging. What he can't know is her agonizing hope whenever she sees that mechanical claw just piercing the depths, as Sister raises her arms and tries to grab on. He doesn't know, I, about her desperation, her grit, as she pushes through the dark silence of the sand, trying to hold on. She doesn't know, Sister, if she'll make it, if I will see her emerge from under the sand, hanging from that mechanical arm, flying over that little world of dolls and toys, trying to withstand the forces willing her to fall. She doesn't know if it's ever going to happen, but she keeps trying, because she wants to be remembered.

37

Home Beneath the Mountain, 1983

GRANDMA SLEEPS ON THE BOTTOM bunk; Sister sleeps on the top. A new bed's appeared in the room, by the window. Same floral carvings, similar design, alpine-style with a twist. This is I's bed.

Sister has had the bunk bed to herself for several years, and she chose the top bunk. She sleeps with an emptiness below her, and nearly every night, she shatters the quiet of the Home Beneath the Mountain with her screams. When I hears her screaming, he automatically sits up in bed. Then he lies back down and covers his head with the pillow.

Sister's screams are always preceded by whimpering that borders on crying. But the crying never happens; those whimpers turn to breathlessness, and then to screams. If I hears her whimper, he jams the pillow over his head, so when she explodes into screaming, it's background noise.

Every night, her screams seem to worsen. They pass through the window, over the flowerbed of the condominium complex, and slam into the mountain, then return, enfeebled, to the room.

Sister screams a scream of terror, of an animal being butchered.

I knows Sister dreams about Father every night.

He also dreams about Father every night, but he doesn't speak of this.

Yet it's Father's voice, half-screaming, that plunges into the room at night, trying to soothe Sister's anguish. It arrives from behind the closed door, from across the hall, the bedroom where Mother and Father sleep.

Sister sees Father inside her dream and screams a butchered scream. Outside her dream, Father's voice arrives and calls her name to calm her. I jams the pillow over his head to keep from hearing.

When Grandma comes for a visit at the Home Beneath the Mountain, she fills the emptiness that Sister sleeps above.

This happens for two weeks, at Christmastime. Afterward, the bed is empty.

At night Grandma fills the room with words. Sister and I turn off their lights; Grandma's light stays on. When the room is dark, Grandma lets Little Girl Grandma slip from her mouth—Sister and I know almost nothing about her. If Grandma happens to forget, they ask for her.

Then, from their beds, they watch her go by.

"I keep her shut away too often," says Grandma.

"She's almost blind by now, when I think of those beautiful eyes of hers."

"She only comes out when you two are here."

"Otherwise, she's ashamed."

Little Girl Grandma now lives only in darkness; she wanders around the room, she hops, sings ditties, does somersaults, jumps on the beds, says whatever she likes.

When Little Girl Grandma is there, the room becomes boundless: a home of many rooms, with long, flowing damask curtains and servants who were always there. And tutors who taught her to say and do what one must say and do. It wasn't beneath the mountain, Little Girl Grandma's home: it was in the historic center of Rome, and that was so long ago, a past that no one recalls.

Then, when she hears Sister and I's breathing grow heavy, Grandma calls Little Girl Grandma back to her; it's time, she says, to let the children sleep. She turns out her light and darkness fills every corner of the room. Some nights, the echo of Little Girl Grandma's voice remains, and kneads its way into their dreams.

Sometimes there's a scream, and sometimes no. At the first whimper, Grandma calls Sister's name, and often, from that whimper, Sister slips back into sleep.

38

Home of the Wardrobe, 2006

IN THE MIDDLE OF THE room, you'll see a cheap, wooden table and three place settings, plate, silverware, red paper napkin to the side. Checkered tablecloth, an autumnal feel. Unmatched glasses, brightly colored, a pop of color, the aftertaste of a summer home.

You'll see Wife—not wife yet—straightening the place settings after Little Girl's somewhat haphazard arrangement. Knife and fork are now parallel, the napkin refolded in a triangle and tucked beneath the fork.

The breadbasket now hiding the stain.

Wife disappears into the bathroom, comes back out wearing her makeup. She rearranges the place settings slightly, two details, essential millimeter changes.

For a moment nothing happens, with Wife in the kitchenette and pans on the stove. A forty-second pause.

Wife's pace now quickens; she takes two separate actions. She opens the door to the wardrobe room, closes it, then heads to the door to the apartment. She opens it. She steps to one side for I, who comes in, smiling, with a small bouquet.

They kiss each other on the cheek. I's jacket winds up on the couch.

Now the door to the wardrobe room opens; Little Girl makes her entrance. She walks toward I, her hand an unholstered pistol, ready for civilities; she squeezes I's hand and pulls the trigger of her name.

Little Girl cuts a distinctive figure, back straight, T-shirt clearly a sign that she's no baby.

Under the table, five feet now: two pairs and one unmatched foot.

The unmatched foot is smaller, in a yellow and blue striped sock. It's hiding behind a chair leg, catlike, barely poking out, staring, curious, vigilant, ready to pounce. A creature with two heads: this is one, and the other, above the table, with Little Girl's face.

One of the pairs of feet is in stockings. And shows dark red toenails. These feet are more rounded than tapered, in keeping with the calves above them, solid and neat. Both soles are planted, unsurprisingly, on the floor. The feet are parallel, the toes relaxed.

The other two feet are hidden inside the carapaces of I's shoes. The two turtles—with dark shells—are joined at the front, one on top of the other.

A freeze-frame of this follows for the next half hour. The parallel feet in stockings, the cat hiding behind the left leg of the chair, the two turtles, head on top of head.

Then everything is back in motion.

The feet in stockings break formation: the painted toes come alive, raise their heads. One foot sits on top of the other awhile, or peeks out from behind the other, hooking an ankle. The right foot rises on tiptoe, the left tips back and forth.

The two turtles open and close formation. Not shifting all that much, but steadily cheerful.

Only the cat stays still, crouching.

Now and then the feet in stockings disappear from the frame, are gone a couple of minutes. The turtles remain, kept in check by the staring cat.

An hour or so goes by; the cat disappears along with the feet in stockings. The two turtles, now alone, shift, venture into new territory, exploring along irregular paths.

Then the picture returns as it was: five feet, two pairs steadily moving, the cat behind a different chair leg but the two turtles always in its sights.

A short while later, on the balcony, three bodies lean on the rail.

I in the middle, Wife on his right, up to his shoulders, hanging onto his arm. Seen from behind, from the Home's point of view, Wife could be one of his wings, tucked in for now, ready to unfurl. The silhouette, in the dark, seems like a maimed angel, an angel with a missing a wing.

Little Girl stands slightly apart, on I's left, a fissure between their two bodies. A few centimeters, certainly less than five, maybe only three.

Wife pushes against I, just barely, to close the gap. I doesn't resist, accepts this joining, Little Girl's shoulder against this arm.

To understand what happens next, you'd need to read the score of I's skin, the rippling that opens his pores. I shivers, and Wife thinks it's from the cold. She pushes on him a little more, her grip protective on his arm.

From the Home's point of view, the angel is now complete. Little Girl is the second wing, though smaller than the right.

It's Wife who did this, with her gentle shove.

And to find out if this angel is real, I would have to climb past the rail and hurl himself over the city.

39

Prisoner's Home, 1978

THE POINT OF VIEW IS at a diagonal. Imagine two eyes, from inside a second-floor apartment, staring at a nineteenth-century villa across the street. The eyes follow a woman walking with a boy—she moves gracefully while he is chomping at the bit, ready to burst out running. They stop before the closed gate, and the boy reaches through the bars, waves, presses his face against the iron.

Keep in mind all the plants on the terrace: they might block the view, but the villa is there, just below, with Rome in the background.

The eyes watch from inside and through a screen of curtains, a cream-colored tulle filter. So owing to this material, the park and mansion are out of focus, as is the dry fountain.

Through the curtains, Rome is a shade of white, a cloud that's lost its sky. The city viewed from the terrace, though, without the tulle, gets its sky back. And all the other colors on the scale: the green of the curtains on the balconies, the yellows and oranges of the buildings. In the distance, the Palazzo delle Esposizioni and the incongruent grandeur of the basilicas of Saint Peter and Saint Paul. The EUR is the horizon every morning for the rising sun.

But the view from the terrace isn't so popular with the

kidnappers; better to look through a curtain. Behind the kidnappers is drywall and behind this is Prisoner—for him the only sun to contemplate is the lightbulb in a teardrop table lamp; there's no EUR, no villa below. The Portuense district, then Via della Magliana, blur together, acoustics, background noise. The Tiber, unseen, makes its way to the sea.

Observed from the apartment, the villa feels largely abandoned. The grounds are overgrown with brush and spreading, choking grass.

The villa has no idea what will become of it. If it's destined to go to ruin or will survive the current building bulimia raging in the neighborhood. If it will continue to be nothing, with only its walls put to use for swastikas and soccer slogans. If it will be a home to mice, a municipal building, a parish, or a shopping center.

Nights, it's a space of conquest, needles in veins, cigarettes and copulation, a spasm of bodies, gasping orgasms: a lake of darkness that gives way to morning's undergrowth, to natural decay. But to the watching eyes, it's still a park, an unexpected ceasefire in a war of concrete.

Those suspended eyes at the second-floor window now observe the small boy beside his mother, who reaches for his hand. It's Mother and I, standing in front of this abandoned park, and within the sights of this white-curtained gaze.

These two, Mother and I, they're not important for the eyes. They don't pertain to History, aren't for or against the Revolution. They're just movement, not reassuring, not particularly threatening. Mother pushes a stroller that I refuses to climb into.

I runs and runs on the sidewalk surrounding the villa;

sometimes he falls, gets back up. If he cries, that's not heard from behind the glass on the second floor. And neither is Mother, if she says something to him when he points down at Testaccio and the distant skeletal frame of the Gasometro.

Mother and I walk around in the park; it's only a day for them, not History. There's nothing more to say, from the current point of view. In the end, these two will go home. To the Underground Home, or perhaps to visit Relatives—both are nearby.

From behind, they're defenseless, the backs of their necks exposed.

| MODULARIO
F. rig. rend. 487 | | MINISTERO DELLE FINANZE
DIPARTIMENTO DEL TERRITORIO
CATASTO EDILIZIO URBANO (RDL 13-4-1939, n. 652) | MOD. BN (CEU)
LIRE 200 |

Planimetria di u.i.u. in Comune di.......▓▓▓▓▓....... via ▓▓▓▓▓ .... civ ▓▓▓▓▓

PIANO PRIMO
H 2.70 m

3

2

B

R

C

1

ORIENTAMENTO

Prot. (Mod. 8) n° 6853 19▓▓▓
Voltura e/o U.I.U. n° 1
IMPORTO £ 50 000

SCALA DI 1:100

Estratto di mappa
1:2000

1 8 SET. 2000   0517 11

| Dichiarazione di N.C. ☐
Denuncia di variazione ☒ | Compilata dal ▓▓▓ | RISERVATO ALL'UFFICIO |

Ultima planimetria in atti
Data presentazione 18/09/2000 - Data ▓▓▓
Formato ▓▓▓ (210x297) ▓▓▓
n. ▓▓▓ sub. ▓▓▓

40

Parallel Home, 1991

THE PARALLEL HOME IS MAINLY a vibration through the walls of the Home Beneath the Mountain. Its lack of words creates a secret immunity that description would only compromise. It's the place where Father goes when he's been missing a long while, and Mother glances at the clock and out the window, to the absent car, not there on the street. It's the thought of this that makes her drop a plate or glass in the sink, makes her fingers bleed while she gathers shards and drops them in a bucket instead of thinking about her husband in a different bed. It's the place on her finger beneath the Band-Aid; when Father does return and goes into the bathroom and asks her about that cut as if it were nothing, she answers that she was distracted; and then she always follows this with a meal, and the blood reappears, escapes its seal, and winds up on the table and in the food.

The Parallel Home isn't something to discuss with the children, so it's only bound to Father's vibrating vocal cords, how at dawn or in the dead of night, that vibration slips beneath the Home's closed door. Usually from their bed, rarely, from the kitchen, the air trembles: I, a teenager, hears it as he lies awake; it collides with his ear, tugs on his head. He knows that sound, knows it speaks of that place. A preverbal language, almost extraterrestrial, Father's voice deprived of language, reduced to a wave. The true language of the species, really, the sound an animal makes, and a cub pricks its ears to.

This is the language Father speaks and that Mother responds to by crying, the second language I hears from the other side of the Home Beneath the Mountain. Mother cries and Father emits those ultrasounds that come in intermittent waves: long waves, then silence, crying slipping through, the vibration again, the crying again, briefer, another ultrasound that Father directs like a laser toward her emotion, toward Mother's liquid sadness. When the emotion has grown necrotic, when the wave has struck with one last jolt, the crying stops, and so does Father. Then I hears the straining mattress springs beneath the two bodies, hears his whispering, also preverbal, though modified for sweetness. But sometimes it's an assault, sex pounds sadness against the wall to make sure sadness is dead, and afterward, grows quiet.

Now it's morning, and Father and Mother are already in the kitchen, having breakfast, and Mother laughs, holds up her bandaged finger. Father is satisfied—even the temperature of the milk is just right. It's Sunday; Sister's still in the room that she and I share, and Mother goes to make the master bed; I stays with Father in the kitchen, dunks his cookie into his cup of milk, a mute, crumbling explosion, one chocolatey piece remaining in his hand. Father talks to him about the Parallel Home, quietly, turning slightly to make sure Mother is still gone. He's smug, tells I that Mother understands—it can be done—it's not like he's taking anything away from her. He sounds more concerned with a boy's initiation than trying to justify himself to his son. When Mother returns, Father gets up, and she puts his cup in the sink.

The vibration in Father's voice will return at dawn, and the crying, and Mother's necrotized emotion once again, and then breakfast. The Parallel Home will return, a space that's just a bed, no measurements, no land registry, no floor, and where the bed ends the sinkhole begins, dislocated in some imprecise urban space, pavement, street signs, fixtures, and buildings, but also sidereal, freed from gravity. It will return. And so will bandages and broken dishes in the sink and cookies turned to pulp in mugs; and secrets will return, and I's fear of being alone in the same room with Father, and then looking into Mother's eyes and not saying a word.

41

Family's Elegant Home, 2018

With the door open, I mainly sees walls.

To empty a home is to give it back its walls, its masonry skeleton, while living there denies this construction, turns it into a space (the pictures hanging on the walls say: "Look at us, not at what's behind us").

Emptying a home is an attention-seeking moment for nails, which are designed to live hidden: only now do they reveal themselves to the light. They emerge from the walls like snail antennae, protruding to see: they're the eyes of the brick; they see that everyone has gone.

The entryway is a crucifixion field. Rather than leaving these nails bare and gasping on their own, Wife used them to crucify the words I left for her every morning for years, on slips of paper, before he walked out, and shut the door behind him. Sentinel words—they watched over the apartment in his place while Wife lay helpless and abandoned in bed. Each note, I tore from a tower of Post-its.

He wrote, "Amore," while standing with his backpack on, or just in his boxers, feet bare, while he sat, trying to shake off sleep. Sometimes he returned when he was already out by the elevator, so Wife wouldn't wake up without that welcome committee. His handwriting tells all, the EEG of his mood, saying more about I than what he's written. Nothing major, of course, just welding love and practice together, reaffirming the promise of the future, postponed till dinnertime. Some days, more explicitly sentimental.

I'm going, Amore, see you tonight.

Going to the post office, won't be back before 7, love you.

The walls—what I sees as he steps inside—are an exhibition of paper rectangles, butterflies pinned to the walls. I's words wriggling, still resisting, just barely: the air lifting their edges, flight an agonized intention.

Good morning, Amore, says the crucified butterfly, *call you around lunchtime.*

So lucky to have you—you make me feel alive. The nail through the signature.

Amore mio, can't find the car keys—have you got them?

Every one of I's words, writhing. His sentences, trying to fly, but now more of a confused death flutter. Or already dead, the scene peaceful, the soul having flown from the words.

I ate too much cake, sorry Amore, call you when I leave.

Every room is the same landscape of words contradicted by action. The nail—Wife—has merely crucified the lie.

The walls of Family's Home are the gallows of an ending love.

Wall after wall, I takes his own dead words down off the cross.

He does this with quick motions, trying for a clean tear.

Every note has its handwriting of the day. And its own color, and vibrancy of ink.

I lets his sentences fall one upon the other, into a shoebox. Probably, he'll leave them in the Home, before he goes away for good. The new tenants will find them, or the workers cleaning and whitening the space.

They'll open the box and sense how much life is still contained in a dying thing.

42

Home of the State, 1997

Let's consider the three lives of a modest city hall in a town outside Turin, and in the end, move to imagining I inside, alone, lying on a bed.

First, then, the outside stairs: eight normal-sized steps, a typical entrance to a State building. Inside is a stairway leading to the second floor. The steps are worn from long use: evidence of an involuntary piety, the climb to the realm of records, numbered documents, files.

The rest of the building consists of rooms. The number and layout don't matter. Labyrinthian. The redundancy and anonymity, narcotic-like, in this place of power. The white walls, the tan floor tiles, the metal desks with painted tops, the PVC ductwork, all bring on nausea and the effect of morphine.

After imagining this city hall, let it go; replace it with an elementary school.

150

By revising the town plan, the city center is now decentralized. And since townhall was the fulcrum of power, now this power is off-kilter, unstable. So new people are voted into office. Put the center back where it belongs, the city will return to its proper balance.

And so the move: tons of files, desks, and staff relocated to a new glass building that was put up without a competitive bidding process but with guaranteed parking. Panoramic elevators, voice recognition.

So now the old town hall building is to be an elementary school. Fluorescent lighting and its constant drugged effect, chipped floor tiles, kilometers of wiring inside and outside the walls, clearly not up to code.

So the ensuing era for the building is this: the steady hum of the municipal machine alternating, by the bell, with silence and the din of children. Rather than repainting the walls (due to a lack of funds), they're hidden beneath drawings in crayon or marker of families, animals, and natural landscapes. Maps, too, make their contribution: the world, at least the one that's scaled, provides an alternative to the defeat on the local level.

But the labyrinth is basically the same. The offices have become classrooms, the large metal desks making way for smaller Formica versions. But the hum of the municipal machine, the building's tinges of breath remain. And after six o'clock, after the front door is locked, the state machine starts to gurgle. Inaudible at first, rising quietly, from the foundation. A growing sound, spilling into the building, overwhelming every floor tile in every room. The unseen master of the place: seething in the quiet, churning up a miasma of filed records, marriages, births, divorces, deaths, suffocating in the white rows of registers, archived cases mangled with stamps.

—

Now take away the school.

Imagine a crack in the ceiling of a classroom. Then a cave-in, the ceiling opens, crashes, dust, rubble, broken tile and bricks. Don't worry—no children harmed or killed—it's the middle of the night. A terrorist attack carried out by the ghost of power. Picture it: a couple of short articles in the local papers, some old council members' mouths watering over the upcoming elections, and piles of complaints in files at the new town hall, open records, stamps, stamped letters.

Now step back inside the building. Imagine the damaged roof, the general state of decay, the hushed churning odors of the machine. Imagine an abandoned labyrinth, no mystery, no punishment, no way out. Doors closed, rooms sealed off, no children, no staff, no desks of any kind. And everything no doubt covered in dust.

Now imagine a small room, eight meters square, with a window, first a space for various filings, complaints, and bankruptcies, then, with the school, a janitor's closet. Put a twin bed in there— no—a metal frame and mattress. Add an orange blanket, cheap, acrylic, constantly chemically warm.

Now put a pale green Formica chair beside the bed; set an old metal reading lamp on the chair, and a pair of folded glasses, a book, and an address book. On another chair, nearby, an old TV, a discontinued model, black and white, whisker-antennae raised.

Now to the head resting on the pillow. It's I of course. His hair is long. Shiny with oil, dirty. His cheeks are covered in the peach fuzz of a twenty-year-old attempting a beard.

He's asleep, breathing deeply, inhaling the odors of the building, swelling with defeat. His bronchi are saturated with bureaucracy, repetition, and brown chromatics. Outside is everything else, in motion, as always. This is I's official assignment from the State in lieu of military service, his quarters, his debt to the community.

It's Sunday. I opens his eyes; the nearby hall bell rings at eight o'clock. He pads out of his closet-room in his bare feet, headed for the bathrooms down the hall, and the kid-sized toilets.

After his shower (a showerhead installed over a squat toilet), he goes back to his room, heels beating time to the state nothingness of this place, all the locked doors, the marble stairways, the stark ceilings, faded walls. I leaves all this outside, shuts the door to his room. He lies down on the bed, towel around his waist, the rest of his body beaded from the shower. It's his first apartment—his first home, really, as a young man, almost a man, with the euphoria of leaving provincial life behind. I feels a sort of alienated affection for the State: institutionalized gratitude.

He picks a book up off the floor, reads a few lines, sets the book back down; he gets up, turns on the TV. Everything is in black and white, so even the present has the flavor of the past, seems like an old movie or a worthwhile destination. I dozes off, half-naked. Soon he's awake—or maybe it's much later—a voice, a desperate cry, from the TV. A man with thick, white eyebrows, shouting, "We've lost a poet!" then saying it again, then again, desperate, before a coffin, people everywhere. "A poet should be sacred!" the man sputters, wracked with emotion. I sits up, wondering when all this occurred.

43

Underground Home, 1977

It's a midsummer day, hot like so many others. All around, Rome seems exhausted. It comes to life a bit in the early morning, and then in the evening, when it's cooler. The rest of the day it glowers in its heat and stays quiet. A breeze blows through in irregular puffs, is already gone, teasing a return, making the wait unbearable.

The birds cry sharply, a knife across the windows.

The square patch of sky between the buildings is a screen where nothing occurs. Only minimal color variations, blue to white, then back again. The sunset is tinged slightly, just barely, with red.

I is alone, in the cement yard with Turtle.

Perhaps Grandma, Sister, Mother, and Father are inside, but for I, inside doesn't exist now. The inside he likes is everything outside the Home.

For I, all that exists is Turtle: she's a hemisphere moving in space, not just a shell. He learns from her that the world is a shifting body.

I likes to race Turtle in the yard. He always gives her a slight head start: he watches as she scuttles off, beating time with her bones. Then he starts to crawl, though he's known how to run for a while.

He always skins his knees on the cement, sometimes draws blood. But he doesn't feel it, it doesn't hurt, is all a part of the lesson. Competition demands this ritualistic pain.

I isn't interested (as perhaps Turtle might be) in racing to the other side of the cement yard; he's not interested in winning.

What he wants to do is ride her.

So he crawls to reach her, and shrieks like a pirate. When she first hears him coming, Turtle flails a bit, but then she stops and lets him climb on, his legs straddling her.

And they set off, and taking flight like this is the most natural thing in the world.

From a kitchen window overlooking a balcony, someone stands watching the unbounded journey of a turtle and a toddler.

44

Underground Home/Sea Branch, 1988

It's a coastal concept: the realization that the sea generates profit. In urban terms, this means speed of construction and concrete. In social terms, this means the concept of the vacation updated for capitalism: not the villa but the rented condo, not a few pale people in nice clothes, but everyone, dressed alike and tanned according to one's allotted melatonin.

The landscape: your typical beach resorts. Rows of umbrellas, three layers of wellness plantations, two in June and September, four around Ferragosto. Not the intense colors of the early 1970s, more faded now, indicative of an aging tourist model. But still subdivided by color blocks and corresponding, according to a precise social algorithm, to a membership and a restricted area of the capital: Rome is sixty kilometers away. And the Underground Home (to be precise) is eight more besides. This is its summer branch.

Within each color block—blue for the Little Mermaid Resort, bright green for the Aurora—the distance from the water and shoreline defines a clear internal social geography: professionals in the front row with a sea view, and everyone else behind. The beach huts, few in number and at the rear, cordon off the resort and reflect the privilege of those vacationers up front, as they're the only ones with access to these rectangular wooden structures. Each hut has a number painted on the door, and the same number on a sea-creature key ring. Hanging inside these huts are swimsuits and towels and all the necessary entertainment equipment, from sand buckets to donut floaties, crossword puzzles, and an inflatable raft and foot pump.

This is the view from the street, looking over the low wall. I's beach umbrella is on the right, halfway down the second row. Indistinguishable from the others, of course, when seen from here. A large, faded green hat.

The Home is a hundred meters from the beach: ground level, two bedrooms and a kitchen, a small garden with blooming roses. Two months at a rip-off price to rent this sea-view cement. But a debt Grandma pays every year to atone for bringing her son into this world. And in retaliation, Father insults her when anything bad happens. He wishes her dead; then—he says—it'll be better. When they all go to bed, Grandma starts to drink. Sometimes she falls down in the hallway, in the middle of the night, and all I hears is a thud. No cry, just a dead body rising again and heading off to sleep.

But what's more important to I is the empty space between the beach resorts. This is the gray zone, where privilege dissolves, where the locals spend their time. Isolated spots, each with a beach umbrella, and a sense of despair or having too much fun. A lot more cigarettes, rumpled overalls, pale skin, T-shirt-sleeve tan lines. In other words, a scene that's not as slick: provincial life on the coast, not a vacation by the sea, the beach an outlet for mothers, the undressed sequel to apartment life.

What separates the gray zone from the resorts: fencing. A bamboo screen, actually, that shields the Romans from seeing the bodies of the locals, their salad bowls, their eggplant parmesan, the sauce on their faces. Basically, the fencing shields metropolitans from boring everyday life: instead, for a resort's end-of-month fee, they get an exclusive sort of boredom under a beach umbrella, with a book and newspaper, the truncheons of the ruling class. Straightforward prose lies hidden behind the fence, and so the fiction is preserved, the cerebral cortex rested. Not to mention the benefit to the ears: you can avoid the terrible Italian, the local yokels' Romanesco.

It's past this fencing where I feels at ease. He comes here on his own, with a soccer ball, an object banished at the resort. He does kick-ups, counting out loud until the ball drops, and begins again at "One," changing his foot, sometimes using his head. Until someone approaches, horns in and takes the ball, though I doesn't mind. And a pickup game begins.

This only happens in the late afternoon, the time of the locals, scooters buzzing along the shore, crowding the sidewalks. I waits for them, the fourteen-year-olds riding them; he's jealous of their brawling faces, their hands nicked from working on radiators and ignition coils, wrenches in repair shops, their oil-smeared fingers. And he's jealous of their nicknames, which is all he'll ever know them by. He's jealous of what he considers to be their life, the justice they wield, stealing bikes in the historic center, painting them, selling them by the resort, the sneers on their faces. And then they tell him, "Ciao bello," and zip off on their scooters, and he's never sure when they'll return. No sign of them in the historic center, no sign of them at the gelato shops. They hang out past the station, six kilometers from the sea—maybe—in the housing projects along Via Ardeatina, some place along there.

45

Home of the Wardrobe, 2005

THE HOME OF THE WARDROBE has been reduced to a bed, with a window for consolation. It's the larger bed, intended for Wife—who's not yet Wife—where she lies all day; Little Girl's bed, in the wardrobe's opposite hemisphere, has been empty for weeks.

Little Girl always enters the apartment at sunset. Her rhythm is tied to the sun: when the sun goes down behind the mountains, it lifts her to the eighth floor. The final acceleration, the mysterious quickening as the sun suddenly drops, often occurs while the elevator rises, almost as if the sun itself is a counterweight to her light body.

The sun disappears and Little Girl opens the door. Soon after, the door closes again, and the elevator slides down the shaft to the ground floor with Wife's father, Little Girl's grandfather, inside: his role is to open the apartment door for his granddaughter and leave her there a few hours with her mother. Soon his car pulls away from the other parked cars, onto the street; in a couple of hours, it will reappear on the opposite side of this same street.

—

Little Girl mainly stands by the bed and watches Wife sleep. She doesn't touch the mattress with her legs, doesn't even graze it. She stands a few centimeters away, half a tile's distance, a safety measure, her drawbridge, her escape route.

Sometimes she takes a chair from the other room, sets it a slight distance from the bed, and sits down. She doesn't always look at her mother—she gets distracted. Not by anything in particular—the window sometimes—she sees the Alps, and when it grows dark, she sees herself in the glass; other times, she sees things in her mind.

More often than not, however, she gets lost in the landscape of her own skin: she investigates the texture of her forearm, her hand, the downy hair she sees. She spreads the tiny pore craters piercing her skin, the point where a hair breaks through the scaly grid. She draws close, leaning her face over that fine, intricate, yet oddly proud plantation.

After studying this a long time, Little Girl raises her head, looks somewhere else. She twists and feels her neck muscles and back muscles, and this returns her to the room, to its space, floor tiles, furniture.

Before her, on the mattress and bedframe, Wife is almost always a sleeping body. Head a weight on the pillow, face contorted, in unrestful abandon.

The head of this body is practically bald, except for a few patches of hair. The eyebrows are only something to remember, a neglected brow-ridge relief, two suggested lines protruding over the ocular cavities. The overall impression here is one of sweat—sweat that dulls the skin rather than giving it luster, sweat that crumples the sheets. And what's plain to see: death is attempting to plunder an almost abandoned body. And it's clearly difficult, in death's presence, to say *mother*.

And she also can't speak of the illness, can't say *tumor*, can't say *cancer*.

Saying these words, letting them slip from her lips, would help: then Little Girl would have something to work with, the mechanics of words that she might study, and not just a body in a bed that she ignores.

But Little Girl has only her own forearm to observe, the mysterious downy hair that testifies to the power of life but only if she looks at this, and this alone. Otherwise, there's just a desolate landscape, the body of her mother, what they call the result of treatment, or the struggle for life.

Most of the time, this is all that happens, just this exposure: daily access to a sense of the end, pouring straight out of her mother's sick body. A weaning with no substitute formula. Most of the time, Little Girl only hears the click of the lock, the door opening, and her grandfather coming in, coming close, whispering it's time to go. Then they both approach the bed where Wife lies. The grandfather kisses the top of his daughter's head, then gestures to Little Girl, encourages her, and Little Girl almost always reaches and touches her mother.

Later the door shuts; Little Girl lets her grandfather help her on with her coat: he's taken it off the coatrack where it hung beside his daughter's wig. Now everything ends with two bodies in the elevator: Little Girl presses the lobby button, and the rest is habitual, repetitive, the mechanics of a heavy body falling, controlled by cables.

—

But then there are other times when Wife, quite simply, opens her eyes, and they focus on Little Girl sitting in a chair at the end of the bed. And so the drawbridge lowers. Not much more to say about what happens next, just that it does. The bridge lowers, the plank is now on the bank, and Little Girl crosses over. She climbs onto the bed, clambers toward the middle, and stretches out beside the body of her mother. No drama, no tears. It's all matter of fact: Wife asks if her homework's done, and Little Girl pretends to sleep.

26239

MINISTERO DELLE FINANZE
DIREZIONE GENERALE DEL CATASTO E SERVIZI TECNICI ERARIALI

NUOVO CATASTO EDILIZIO URBANO

Planimetria dell'immobile sitato nel Comune di
Piano
Allegata alla dichiarazione presentata all'Ufficio

piano PRIMO

CORT. COMUNE

1

2

INGR.
h 2.70 m

Altra U.I.

BAGNO

3

CUCINA

ATRIO
COMUNE

4

GIARDINO

Scala 1:200

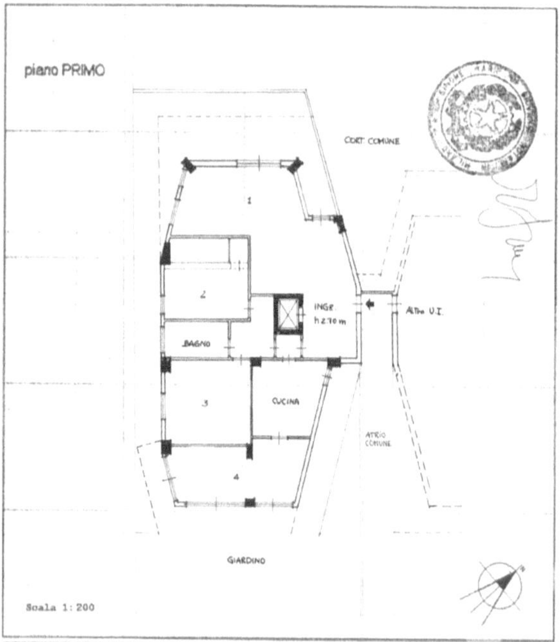

SPAZIO RISERVATO PER LE ANNOTAZIONI D'UFFICIO

DATA
PROT. N.

Ultima planimetria in atti

46

Home of Poet's Secret, 1981

WHAT'S SO STRIKING IS HOW dark it is in here. Now and then the door rises, and the darkness gives way, in a horizontal band of light.

A furtive view: cars parked haphazardly. State-seized cars, detained, locked up, mysteries, ongoing investigations.

No matter how much you strain, there's no seeing the Home of Poet's Secret; it's sealed inside this darkness. It could be a coupe, an Alfa Romeo; the darkness holds onto this, as does the entry, with Poet's name, in the logbook. It's his last car, and has survived him, left him lying in the mud, in Idroscalo.

The garage door goes down, the thud devours the space, darkness swallows the parked cars. Meanwhile, Rome is lit up, dazzling.

In the background runs the Appian Way, as it has for over two thousand years.

What we might discuss first about the Home of Poet's Secret is what distinguishes it within the world of commodities. Its name is Alfa Romeo GT 2000, to which the epithet "Veloce"—fast—must be added, despite its current condition. But it's precisely this use of adjectives—a stylistic preference, a weakness—that's key to Poet's pride, the absolute record holder of the space-time continuum, champion of the pedal to the metal, unparalleled burner of engines.

What's more important to this particular case, though, is the metal plate with embossed lettering affixed to the bumper: Rome K69996. It's this code that has set the cogs of the State in motion, with no escape for the Home of His Secret, that is, before Poet's been identified.

The term "Poet," though, is disembodied, disallowed: not among the professional options the State has listed. So "Professor" has been inserted in the logbook and on the document drawn up when the Home of His Secret was impounded, a term identifying a particular class, and the only detail above suspicion here.

So moving on: the color of the Home of His Secret is metallic gray; the frame has visible damage, though not extreme. The interior is natural leather colored Texalfa, so faux leather; this is Poet's ill-concealed, begrudging tribute to the general enthusiasm for widespread affluence.

The official contents of the Home of His Secret, the certified items, are listed below (with the requisite signatures at the bottom), creating a sort of bureaucratized versification:

Road tax stamp;
Proof of insurance;
3 keys for ignition, doors, other;
1 emergency triangle plus case;
1 jack;
1 tire iron;

1 automotive wrench;

1 spare tire.

Everything signed (three different signatures) and registered, at the top of the page, by the Carabinieri Legion Detective Squad.

What's not on the list doesn't pertain to the world of objects. It can't be found on the front or back seats, under the hood, inside the trunk, under the floor mats.

What's not here, not written in this report, is his secret—the chassis, axle shaft, wheel rim cup: only these know what happened, but they can't testify. They are his secret, carried about on four wheels. Out in the open now, in full light, the sun hitting the glass and metallic hood. The door coming down behind, over the parked cars, immersing them once more in darkness.

Outside, on the cement, stands a young woman; it doesn't matter if she's alone or not. What matters is that this woman has come for the car that is her due, her inheritance. What matters most of all is that this is a restitution, as a State-recognized office has written and signed off on.

Under the May sky gaping over Rome, the woman makes Poet's Secret sing to the revving engine, through the sprawling suburban streets, headed for EUR, never coming near the city's historic center. It doesn't matter if she's actually listening to this song—the interior of the coupe is flooded with it, the upholstery soaked in it.

An unlistenable song. Poet's lament. Poet, whose heart burst inside his rib cage when that car—whisking through the streets of Rome to the first hints of summer—drove onto his body, and dragged back and forth several times, with its 1,500 steel kilograms. That song is his secret, and also that bursting, three-quarters of the way through the twentieth century, a few meters from where the

Tiber becomes the sea. A public and private song that no one can sing because it has no words.

Save one—universal, piercing—spreading in that space, a painful echoing in the wheels: a final wheezing from Poet, reduced to a body dying like an animal, beaten, on a November night, crying "Mamma" up at the sky.

47

Home of Happiness, 2009

It's a space of absolute happiness, the union of two people in marriage. As such, it goes without saying, it should stand outside all cadastral concerns, should evade dimensions, permits, utility contracts, maintenance.

In the present case, happiness is contained within a public space, which by definition renders every single emotion a statistic, dampens emotion in protocol, stores it in records, eventually burying it in dust. Or amplifies it, as I thinks at the moment, as a point of national pride.

Not much to describe here, except the stale echo, the austerity, of a council chamber. A long table against one wall, with an ochre-colored tablecloth. And a microphone on the table, the cord running under the cloth (and lifting it somewhat, showing the worn wood beneath), and then plugged into an extension cord.

As for the rest: an Italian flag dangling lazily in the early-summer heat, beyond the window, on the wall of a modest but stately municipal building just outside Turin city limits, twenty-three kilometers from the Family's Home, with this room as its embassy.

Inside, on the wall behind the table, the photo of a president of the Republic, halfway through his term—so the photo is only slightly discolored—and then in the middle of the room, dark gray plastic chairs set in a ritualistic but fairly typical manner, good for all sorts of celebrations, including this one. An aisle down the center divides this secular space into two naves.

In front of the table, two chairs and two more witnesses.

The car that arrives is the Self-Propelling Home, the technical device appointed to take I on the one side and Wife with Little Girl on the other, and turn them into a family. The reaction has been triggered, the metamorphosis has been successful, so the time has come to document this, to affix the seals of the State.

Now everything is quite clear, as three car doors open, rolling out the carpet to three different people. Time has overthrown the genetic tyranny of resemblance that held Wife and Little Girl together and left out I; the three faces of these three different people hold the same expression: amazement, impudence, and determination. Little Girl carries the flag of this successful miracle.

It's the same car as always, not any cleaner, not any nicer, no fictionalized rental. Just a diagonal parking job, in one of the rectangles provided. And to think that only an hour and a half earlier, inside Family's Home, they were showing one another their clothing, sailing off barefoot down the hall, Wife with a more traditional modesty —and a carefully chosen dress—and Little Girl searching for just the right elegance to make that day a kind of reparation ritual. I, instead, with little to show them, mainly asking for help: him in the kitchen, sitting near the sink, Wife and Little Girl on either side of him, Wife, her makeup barely begun, tying the knot to his tie, with little expertise and great hilarity. I just letting her, knowing the absurdity here would be revealed forever in the photos along with this tenderness, and imprinted with Wife and Little Girl's laughter, with them gazing at him and his foolish knot, from a distance, then running up to kiss him.

Meanwhile, the flag ripples in the wind and the yellow building is incandescent in the sun.

I stands by his chair, across the table from the suntanned mayor. Around I's neck: his tie with its clumsy knot. The relatives of the bride have taken their seats on the plastic chairs arranged by the town clerk.

As for Mother, Father, Sister, and Relatives, there's no point in looking for them among the others.

So the picture here is that half the room pertaining to I is empty, and the other half is full.

Those present are in nice clothes, about thirty people, a dozen children, all elegant, though some are wearing shorts. For the sake of decency and symmetry, some guests move to the other side of the room.

Now turning to the entryway.

Wife walks in, on her father's arm, a concession to tradition, an essence of the sacred sprinkled on top.

I stands alone in the middle of the scene, waiting.

Now imagine how he must be feeling, his thoughts that his solitude is over.

The glorious, blasphemous thought that he's happy, that he's saved.

Now say no more. Let the record show that all this did occur.

48

Home of Nonexistent Grandfather, 1980

THE APARTMENT COULD BE ON the seventh floor, could be on the tenth. Anyway, from up there, everything looks distant.

A place mainly of closed doors; if one is open, I hasn't seen it. A front door, and two names by the doorbell and a doormat with the picture of a dog. Only an adult can open this door, or two children pushing together: it's heavy, reinforced, ten centimeters thick. A lady stands on the threshold and looks at Father and Mother and then lower, at Sister and I: she's pretty, has red hair, a knee-length skirt.

The red-haired lady leads them into a large room. Her hips sway, as do the rhombuses on her skirt; I watches them from behind, kites wheeling in a swelling sky of cloth.

The room is entirely glass, three windows in a row; hard to tell where the apartment ends and the city begins.

On the left, when coming in, there's a space created by a blue couch and two easy chairs: a room within a room. Across from the couch, a TV, turned off, sitting on a stand with the remote control beside it.

On the floor of this space, a red rug.

Nothing on the couch or rug; the TV screen has just been dusted. They step into the room, and appear deformed in the convex glass, Sister, Father, Mother, and I, the red-haired lady ahead of them, and she goes to the other end of the room, next to the dining room table.

The table's been set for eight, though it's only 11:00 AM. There's a man sitting at the table; he's wearing glasses; his shirt collar is open, tufts of hair showing; the gray hair on his head is neatly combed.

Then two girls come into the room, both around ten, though they don't appear to be twins. They politely shake hands. They say "Hello" to Father and Mother, and "Hi" to Sister and I. They turn to the man and call him "Dad."

He gets up, pushing his chair back with his legs, and the table shakes. A small concert of glasses, though nothing breaks. The red-haired lady leans over the wine glasses, more kite-flying in the sky.

The man ignores Father's outstretched hand, which grows stiff; the man nods toward Sister and I, and says, "So here are the Grandkids."

"The Children," Father says. And pulls his hand back, a fist now at his side.

"I'm Grandpa," the man says to the two of them. He extends his hand.

Sister and I shake it, one after the other.

"You must be their mother," he says, turning to Mother. To Father he says, "You've gotten older."

"Yeah, I was sixteen," Father answers.

"Eighteen," Grandfather says.

"Sixteen." Then Father says, "And you're still a liar."

The red-haired lady turns to the two girls and says, "Take them out to the balcony, to look at Rome."

No one moves. Even Rome remains still, watching this scene play out.

Soon it's time for lunch, earlier than planned; Father and Grandfather sit far apart. The red-haired lady talks with Mother; they're almost the same age, but Mother doesn't wear lipstick or perfume or heels.

A couple of mouthfuls, and the two girls take Sister and I over to the space with the blue couch. They all sit on the floor, so they don't see the table. They stay on the rug, as though in a trench, while beyond the couch, nearby, grenades keep exploding as Father and Grandfather shout back and forth.

The two girls have freckles on their faces, the first thing I always notices about someone. Maybe they're smiling; I doesn't notice. He only sees their freckles, their orange hair, and their white legs under their skirts, knees slightly pink.

They're not especially nice, but they methodically tend to Sister and I.

There's a board game on the floor, and they toss the dice and move their pieces.

All that's said, or all I remembers is, "Your turn."

Everything else comes from the adults, and it's thunder. Grandfather's responses to Father are clipped, reduced to essentials. "Don't shout," for instance.

Or: "You're right, you haven't gotten older. You're still sixteen."

Or: "You're pathetic. You have children and you don't know how to live in the world."

Or: "I'm not even sure I'm your father."

Then there's the pounding of a fist on the table, and this is clearly Father. A concert of glasses, and this time, plenty of broken glass. I can't add up the numbers on the dice. The sisters say the total.

Then Mother comes past the couch and tells Sister and I it's time to go. The meal stopped with the first course. There's still pasta in the bowls. But there's also the coffee pot and full cups, to weld together the beginning and end of the meal and avoid the appearance of melodrama, of a reconciliatory meal gone awry. The girls get up politely, make their way over, say goodbye at the door, a tapestry of freckles, saying in chorus, "See ya."

In the car, Father hits the horn, pounds the steering wheel at the green light. Mother focuses on the windshield, and it's unclear if she sees Rome out there, past the glass. I stares at the back of their two necks, stares at the sidewalks, the small, colorful buildings on Via Cassia, and doesn't think. Sister asks questions that settle into emptiness. The only thing I knows is that Grandfather must also be dissolved in acid. But that won't be so hard, since he only just arrived.

49

Home of the Voice, 1994

As seen from an airplane, it would merge with the Home Beneath the Mountain. But it's another hundred meters further south.

It can host one person standing up, two at most if there's an adult and child. It is, in fact, a rectangular plastic booth, with a pay phone. Meaning a receiver on a hook, a push-button panel, and a coin slot.

The most distinguishing feature of the Home is its transparency: the perfect stage for privacy. The resident is on the proscenium; anyone passing by is invited to watch a scene of private dialogue and especially, to observe how those words that are said and received affect the body. Framed inside this vertical box, the resident's physical expression of feelings is on display. Passing through that theater are agonizing loves, hereditary arguments, bedtime stories, ransom demands, new names for babies, school grades.

Sometimes a whopping lie makes someone jump inside the vertical box. Other times, a person pounds a fist against the transparent wall and insists on a turn. Only then does the person speaking break the fiction and see the world outside. And this person on the phone grows aware of the audience and is awash in shame.

For some time now, though, since most homes started having phones, the vertical box has been deserted. I is by far its major occupant. His time is almost always after dinner, when the cabin is the only light in a general desert. Zero audience members, just a landscape of darkness, closed shutters, a dog or two.

Nearly every night, I comes and slips his coin in the slot. Like the coin lighting up a painting in a church. What's there, suddenly revealed, the money making it exist, if only for the limited time of a set fee.

Every night, I slips that coin in to make a voice exist. He pays to shine a light on the Home of Adultery, where Woman with the Wedding Ring lives with Husband and Twins. His pants pocket swells with coins and his desire for that voice not to end, for the light to stay on. As long as he has coins to insert, the voice exists.

Sometimes this continues for a while: the light shines on the voice and the room. The token slides in and lights up the scene: I can see the easy chair where Woman with the Wedding Ring is sitting, he sees the small side table, the phone she has to her ear. Most of all he sees—lit up, at the center of the stage—the rug where they make love every time.

Woman with the Wedding Ring speaks, whispers, stops if Husband walks into the room or Twins are complaining. She says, "I'm talking to my mother," or "I'm talking to Grandma," her hand over the mouthpiece, suffocating their voices. Soon—or after a while, I digging in his pocket for more coins—the voice resumes, whispering, "*Amore mio*, I have to go."

Then she hangs up, and the light goes off on the fresco.

And darkness engulfs the room; the rug disappears, and along with the rug, the easy chair. And I is back inside the vertical box of the Home of the Voice, happier than when he went in. He pushes the door open, knowing the next day he'll be pushing it to get back inside.

Sometimes, though, the light doesn't shine on the painting; the miracle of payment doesn't take place. Or rather: there's only a flash of light on the scene: The Home of Adultery lasts the moment of a mistake—I can see it for an instant, but then it goes out. I inserts the coin and it's not the right voice, it's the "Hello-Hello-Hello" of Husband. Or even crueler: the "Hello-Hello-Hello" is right, the right voice, but then it says, "Sorry, wrong number," though I, on his end, over and over, keeps saying, "I love you."

50

Underground Home, 2001

FOR FIVE DAYS, TURTLE HAS wandered through the Home; the percussion of her plastron hitting the floor is the irregular metronome beating time in the rooms.

And speeding up or slowing down without prediction. Or suddenly dissolving, when Turtle walks onto the rugs, then returning, after a while, when she's back on the floor tiles. Sometimes, nothing. She's just hiding in something's shadow.

Turtle hasn't gone out to the yard for a week. The sky is a square plug stopping up the space between the buildings.

Of the rooms of the Underground Home, Turtle generally wants to be in the closet where I used to sleep; his pajamas are still in the wardrobe. Turtle's favorite place is under the bed, in the far corner, against the wall.

The closet is swollen with humidity, a primordial space, leading to the origin of things. Turtle enters, as if retaking her place among the other early species. Finally, she slips under the bed and rejoins all the world's early reptiles, from *Casineria* to dinosaur. She pulls her head inside her shell and closes her eyes. She also did this when

I was little, without his knowledge; he'd be asleep when she slipped under the bed: their improvised bunk bed.

The closet ceiling has the same water stains from back then, now in different shapes and sizes, on the entire surface. I would stare up at them, head on his pillow, for hours, like he was watching clouds. He looked for animals, the silhouette of a car, a ball.

These days, if the telephone rings, Turtle runs to the kitchen; the phone sits on a small table.

She always gets there too late, but it doesn't matter anyway.

If the phone rings, it's only two or three times, during the answering service's business hours. Often, after it rings, it starts up again right away. Turtle, on the floor, stretches her neck and stares at the phone until it stops ringing. Then she hides in her shell and stays still.

Above the table, there's a small whiteboard, with a few words written in felt-tip, smeared, hard to read: the ruins of words, relics to interpret. Water; coarse salt; property tax due; a phone number in Rome, the last two digits illegible; shower curtain. In the middle of the board, in a different colored pen: VERANO CEM, FOR CREMATION.

If the doorbell rings, Turtle scuttles down the hall.

Her shell rolls into the shadow of the entryway; she takes long, steady strides, stops a meter in front of the door. She stares at it, from her earlier period. The people out there don't hear anything, though they keep trying. The last few days, this has happened frequently, for much of the day.

They rap on the door with their knuckles. Sometimes, just one person, other times, two; they call Grandma's name, ask if she needs anything, if they can help. The woman's voice is kinder, the man's brusquer, threatening to break down the door. But then they always stop. A door opens, closes.

The phone rings again.

For five days, Grandma's body has been on the bathroom floor, in front of the sink. Her cheek pressed to the tiles, arm outstretched, hand still open.

Barefoot, in a skirt and bra.

Once Turtle saw her, she walked around her every hour. Turtle makes her way around that island that's formed in the middle of the Underground Home; she shapes its contours, her shell beating in mourning, in procession, over and over.

When she goes by Grandma's face, she stops. She looks into Grandma's empty eyes. Turtle is the only one who can do this and not be frightened: she focuses on Grandma's irises, looks into them as if through a keyhole. What she sees, at the end, in the distance, is Grandma's death.

Grandma is in the middle of the apartment; sooner or later someone will break down the door and decide what to do, look for someone to call, say what little there is to say about a body lying in front of a sink.

For now, though, Grandma lies there, and Turtle watches her.

For Grandma, too, these past five days, her home is her tomb.

51

Home Beneath the Mountain, 1984

THE SOCCER FIELD DOESN'T WARRANT much description.

A regulation field, meaning two rectangular halves, two goals, two penalty areas. But a beat-up field, eroded, the grass worn away, and bare dry ground showing. A field that might be called state property, but it falls within the jurisdiction of the Curia; a man in a cassock oversees its use, an earthly reward following catechism.

Any grass by now is pure coincidence. There's been very little for the flying balls, for the cleats—for the all the matches played in that space over the years. Eventually, this grass will disappear: it's only a matter of time, of dribbling and counterattacks.

In the end, matches are arbitrary; no boundary lines mark the beginning and end to the spaces. There were lines once: a white line painted on the grass cut a ball field from a meadow. But time carried this delineated field away, so it's now only a passed-down memory: those who once saw it, retain it, and have a say about corner kicks and offsides. When no veterans are playing, this becomes a negotiation over the invisible. And of course is mainly determined through the exercise of physical strength and fear. The strongest enforces his imagination.

The goals are two octagonal structures without nets; it's pure metaphysics and a touch of rust. In front of each, is an oval-shaped crater carved out from shoes: testimony to the goalie's anxiety and boredom.

The field, then, is slowly going extinct. It's still there, but fading.

I only goes on the field when it's empty, owing to a penchant for solitude and to parental insistence, to not playing by their rules: no church communion, so no playing soccer with others.

And so he comes at dusk. Below the windows, I goes by, ball under his arm.

Sometimes he bounces the ball, to hear something different.

But before he reaches the parish field, he stops at the school building. He peers into the windows, like a margin note on a script. He finds the right window, his own empty desk, as empty as the classroom; this is the tragedy of the bell, especially the final bell: every day is a sentence, returning him to a damaged household. But that's not what I thinks about; he only allows himself to think about his right foot and the ball striking the building in percussive vengeance, his teeth clenched, the conscious ballistics of coming close to the glass, not hitting it, raging against the edifice of the State, the offense of abandoning him, of not keeping him inside.

Then he runs onto the field, ready to be a striker. His match normally goes on about twenty minutes, enough time to miss Father's designated dinner hour. Enough time to see thousands of people sitting in the stands. With him in a Rome uniform, a number 10 on his back. A fantasist: he can out-dribble all nonexistent opponents. He can make a corner kick, between the pole and crossbar, then scream and throw up his arms.

He races around the field, commenting on his every feat. Commentator of his own movements, his own performance, every rout. I has a golden foot—he makes all the difference when played properly on the field: he's the top scorer of an absolute solitude.

In the distance, on a balcony, someone sees him in the gathering darkness. Sees a *giallorossi* boy running in a field, arms raised in triumph. And when the hour strikes, the boy leaves, running, kicking the ball down the street, the playing field going on forever.

52

Prisoner's Home, 1978

As a residence, Prisoner's Last Home is documented in the land registry and has names by the doorbell. What's inside and unseen is a heart pumping infected, putrefying blood into the country.

The décor is an issue. The choice of detail, the cohesion of the furniture, conforming to the tastes of the building. What matters is figuring out how to disappear into the photo, to be forgotten, to dissolve into the big picture.

The Home consists of two bedrooms, a living room, and a kitchen.

The living room has three walls with windows. Plenty of light, transparency, everything outside looks in, or could. So, the décor: above the windows, three rods with white tulle curtains. When they're pulled closed, the outside stays out on the terrace, which is surrounded by a hedge.

The focal point is the large bookcase against the back wall. This bookcase does hold books but isn't full: the volumes are arranged to take up as much room as possible.

You can't see the titles, can't determine an organizing principle. There isn't one, really, just making something look like a bookcase. And if someone entered the room, that's what it would look like. And it would look like a bookcase to anyone peering in from the outside, with the curtains drawn. Even if the curtains were to open and quickly close, like a camera shutter. The image of a bookcase would remain to the eye: the impression of normalcy.

The bookcase sits against drywall; behind this, Prisoner sits on a small cot. The bookcase is the wall of his prison; the words, shut up in the volumes, hold him prisoner. The words are his jailors, wordless, lurking behind the wall.

Twice a day, a small door opens, carved out from the books, and a tray appears with his nourishment. The bookcase is his umbilical cord; Prisoner sucks voraciously because nothing else can keep him alive.

Like any fetus, he's not ready to come out, but he wants to, by instinct. Because like any fetus, he knows and doesn't know that life is out there—what he's straining for with every movement—what will kill him.

Data presentazione: ~~16.07.1960~~ - Data: ~~14.09.2015~~ - n. T277688 - Richiedente: ~~...~~

Allegato "A" al cap. 44085/12190

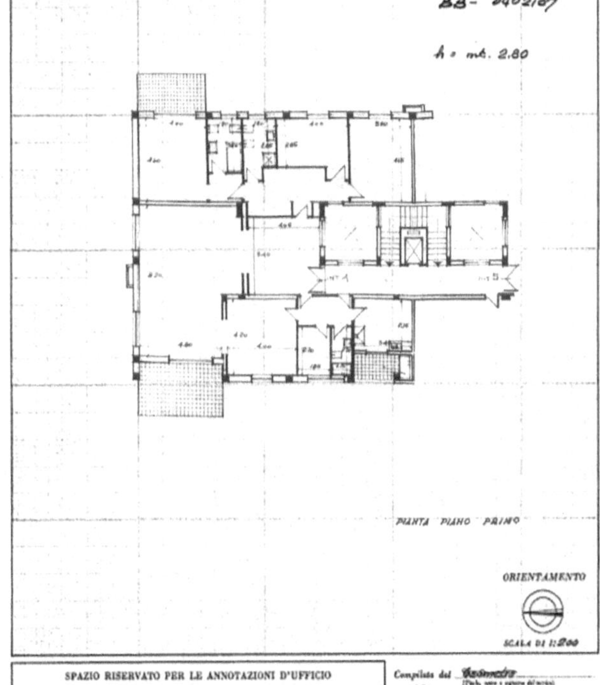

Catasto dei Fabbricati - Situazione al ~~...~~ - Comune di ~~...~~ (H501

Ultima planimetria in atti

Data presentazione: ~~16.07.1960~~ - Data: ~~14.09.2015~~ - n. ~~T277688~~
Totale schede: 1 - Formato di acquisizione: fuori standard (252X377) - Formato stampa richiesto: A4(210x297)

53

Relatives' Home, Home Inside the Fence, Home Over the Rooftops, 2005

The point here is juxtaposition: comparing three Homes, visualizing all three at once.

The first is Relatives' Home. So a hallway, an entryway, Relatives sitting on the far side of the room with the TV on. Then backing up: a small building. Rome all around. Then backing up some more: airplanes in descent, the sea, Fiumicino Airport.

But returning to Relatives' Home, homing in: at the end of the hall, elbow on the table, Mother sits surrounded by Old Relatives and Young Relatives. A choral image, Mother with a tense, pained expression, although pain isn't the main feature here. The fading, late afternoon light paints her cheeks a tired, palliative red; the light imbues her, one might say, with a feminine touch.

In the chorus of Relatives, some sit huddled around Mother at the table, listening—watching her mostly, their neck muscles straining, expressions intent, eyes wide.

Other Relatives—Young Relatives, mainly—stand very close to

these others, so close, they spill over the table until it almost disappears. Two Young Relatives rest their hands on Mother's shoulders.

But while it's a picture of pathos—especially with Mother, her expression, suffering, yet also revealing a restrained joy—the prevailing feeling here is of relief. Averted danger. The worst didn't happen; while it's still the worst, it's only visible in the background.

This is what we see inside Relatives' Home with the door open. As for movement, if there is any, it's marginal. Words are the only animated presence in this scene, lips pressed together, barely perceived whispers.

Among the objects present, we can't help but notice Mother's suitcase, set down near the entryway. Not really a suitcase: a tote bag of some kind, jute-colored. With two leather handles and no shoulder strap. Almost a gym bag, if Mother had something like a gym bag. What is clear, though, sitting there on its own by the entryway, on the speckled marble floor: that bag signals an escape from Father.

And if we were to search for Father in Relatives' Home, we wouldn't find him, though it does seem likely that this gym bag is his.

Now it's time to take the image of Relatives' Home, the crowded, whispering picture around Mother, and juxtapose it with the Home Inside the Fence. Seven hundred kilometers north, 783, to be exact.

In this apartment, Father is a body on a chair at the kitchen table. His head is hidden in his arms; his glasses sit beside his arms; and beneath his arms, a wax tablecloth with a green, abstract pattern.

If the painting were both these two panels, we might come up with a reverse analogy: the table, the scene of pain, the emptiness of the rest of the apartment. The reversal, of course, is the group on the one side, the swarm of Relatives, and absolute solitude on the other. And then a further reversal, outside: the sky of Rome blocked out by buildings, pure orange longing, and on the other side, the fence and reinforced concrete. And not that much to say about the sky of Northern Italy, high over the rectangular buildings.

What really matters in the Home Inside the Fence isn't actually Father, who at the moment is altogether inoffensive. What matters are the walls, the apartment's perimeter, and perhaps the smell. And part of one wall in particular (the space not including the framed prints of some relatively famous paintings), which is smeared with garbage.

Patches in different, irregular shapes. A detailed description doesn't begin to reflect the violence done here: this is a wall that's been stoned, condemned to death, though it's still standing. On the tile floor, what's been pelted: banana peels, a half-eaten, mangled steak, a crumpled milk carton, and more: a shapeless heap of nameless waste of production and consumption. And there on the tiles, the garbage can lies sprawled on its back.

Now one more place, before concluding. The Home Over the Rooftops should now be added to the diptych. So, Paris beyond the windows.

Here, we find I sitting on the floor, beside the image of Father at the table with his head in his arms and Mother in the middle of the whispering chorus of Relatives.

On the rug beside I, in the Home Over the Rooftops, is his cellphone. Not much to add about the role of the phone in the triptych. But worth noting: I's look of misery, his head against the wall.

—

And now the conclusion, about a day later.

Mother on a train, returning: about four hundred kilometers from the Home Inside the Fence; the view out the window, the Tyrrhenian Sea. The bag, the one sitting in Relatives' hallway, now rests between her feet. Her face shows relief, comfort; her escape is coming to a close.

Second panel: Father cleaning, relief on his face, shame in his eyes.

Third: I lets out a scream in bed, his phone in the kitchen, charging.

54

Home of the Wardrobe, 2006

The consistency and duration of the light, a flash of lightning on a detail.

What's lit is a table in the living room in the Home of the Wardrobe. A small, square table, cheap, with a cheap elm-colored varnish. Small, but big enough for Wife and Little Girl: these two at the table make up a family that's indifferent to what might be missing. When there are others, too, as is the case now, they simply add on a prosthesis.

A plastic table—patio furniture. Once white, now yellowing but respectable enough, a solid-based, cross-legged table. Normally on the balcony, now flush with the square table.

This, then, is the focus of the scene: a long table, set for eight. The time in the evening when the outside disappears and the windows reflect what's inside, everything sealed inside a mirror.

What's reflected: a finished meal, dirty plates, some stacked near the mirror's edge, others presumably in the sink, though that's outside the space lit by the lead-glass chandelier hanging over those who are present.

The people sitting around the table barely matter. Of course I's there and so is Wife; it's the start of their time together, the beginning of their relationship; Little Girl might be in bed. Truthfully, the principal figure is Wife—she's the true center of the scene.

The rest are walk-ons—all mainly in their forties—except one. A man, hollow-cheeked, eyes sunken. But smiling, teeth showing, gums receding. The overall impression: a tenderness that's both fierce and defenseless, a knowledge, a reckoning with the end.

The man's nose is hooked; his sweaty bald head shines under the chandelier.

The man is dying; that's clear from the type of kindness those present show him. Their every gesture is a countdown, every generous smile, a screw in the coffin.

No one mentions the tumor, not even one palliative word; but they all know it's destroying his bones, devouring his spinal column.

That word no one says is what joins Wife to this man. It might not be clear—perhaps the others at the table don't realize. But there's a difference in how they look at him: Wife's gaze holds no pity; there's only clarity, precision, as she passes him the bread and says, "Please."

I might notice, but is too distracted by continually saying *I*.

Then in a matter of seconds, it happens. The man raises his glass. The others raise theirs, in collective relief, but the man directs them to set their glasses back down.

He says, "Please," so they won't feel uncomfortable, but their discomfort doubles.

He wants to make a toast with Wife, just Wife.

Now imagine the scene. The two faces, the two glasses,

everyone else suddenly in shadow, secondary to the image, marginal. I is with the others, unseen, in the molasses of darkness overwhelming the light.

The man, staring intently at Wife with his sunken eyes, says the few words which—in a flash—will complete the picture.

He says, "The two of us, we're the luckiest ones here."

This is the flash of lightning, the vision. Entirely unexpected.

In the dark, the embarrassed mass stays quiet, the ridiculous host of the healthy.

55

Home of Escaped Memories

THE HOME OF ESCAPED MEMORIES is a buzzing that won't quit. Even with the crab claw midair, hanging, there's a tension, a suppressed electric impulse, an intention. An apparatus designed to act, to plunge, claw wide open, to vanish into sand, straining, then rise up, a memory I didn't recall now hanging in its grasp.

Working ceaselessly, at night. No light to guide it, working stubbornly, instinctively, even through blackouts. We shouldn't just consider I, unconscious in his sleep, and the all-too-comforting thought that a memory tucked back in place might complete him. We should think instead about the memories themselves, hostages to a Plexiglas box, staring out. Think of the landscape they watch, which they should belong to.

Now the claw lowers, the buzzing increases, grows denser. The claw rests on the bottom, seems to linger a moment, before pushing, pushing. Below, barely below, Sister feels its heavy pressure. The claw is still, is only metal pressed into the sand, but it's cutting off her air. Like every other time, Sister tenses, ready to grab on, to be extracted from oblivion; and like every other time, her effort will be in vain.

There's a clap of thunder, though down here it sounds more like a muffled gun shot. It's the claw bellowing open. Sister has a suitcase, and normally she packs light; but this time if she makes it out, she won't return. She's dressed like a little girl; so—she thinks—I can't possibly fail to recognize her, can't fail to see her pigtails. Inside her suitcase, along with everything else, is a bundle of returned letters, and in these letters, she tells him she loves him, and then there's the one letter she received, the one I sent, in which he says he can't turn back, that she, Sister, is the limb he has to leave behind in the trap, to save himself.

There are also two photos in the envelope, one with the siblings dancing in the kitchen, maybe ten and twelve then, Sister leading, I following, clumsily. And then the other, the second photo, of Sister's balcony, taken from the street, out the car window, with him pulled over after leaving the Home Inside the Fence for the last time—forever—with Wife and Little Girl; not a good shot, timid, partly a coward's farewell, partly an execution.

When she sees the claw piercing the sky, Sister raises a hand, but without conviction. Afterwards she sits back, gives up. She undoes her pigtails, and then the claw is poking beside her; she'd only have to reach out, but she doesn't. And as the claw rises once more, she opens her suitcase, scatters her letters in the sand, turning them to seed, to fertilizer. Then she stops and looks up as the claw disappears and the buzzing fades.

56

Little Girl Grandma's Home, 1982

THE HOME CAN ONLY BE imagined. And only Grandma knows it—strictly speaking, it wouldn't exist at all, if Grandma didn't describe it to Sister and I at bedtime.

So the Home is held up with words rather than walls. Its lintel is the alphabet, its concrete, Grandma's sentences, and it is raised day after day by Sister and I as they lie in bed with their eyes closed.

Punctuation has stabilized the structure: they've used commas as nails to hang pictures; semicolons are for reinforcement as needed, as dowel holes. They've used colons to run pipes and electrical cables through the walls, for water in the pipes and lights in the rooms, to turn the lights on in the kitchen and play songs on the radio. Periods, finally, have fastened things together.

This is how Grandma has shown the Home to Sister and I for many years. While she herself can never go inside. At age twenty, she was forced out the door and told she was never to show her face again. Before all this, for twenty years, she'd been the middle daughter of Rich Couple.

Why all this happened is a secret Grandma tucked inside a strongbox that no longer has a key. But it happened. Since then, the Home is a part of her interior necropolis.

Little Girl Grandma's Home is in the city center. With Rome all around, Grandma tells them, and this is the needle point of the compass. All the rest is circles, falling, forming: one of the smallest runs through the Underground Home. Keep widening the compass, and you reach the sea.

Near Little Girl Grandma's Home is a two-thousand-year-old building, a site of nonstop pilgrimages. It has a circular structure, with Corinthian columns holding up a pediment and portico. And a slightly flattened dome that can be seen from afar; in this dome is a circular aperture, which, from the inside, looking through it, turns the sky to a blue disc: an eye looking in at those walking down below.

From above, the dome resembles a carapace. There's a turtle in the middle of Rome, in among the buildings.

Inside this circular structure, there's nothing. And that's why everyone wants to see it, Grandma tells them. There's something inside here that no one understands—you can't even pray in here. No one really knows what to do; they all just walk around under that wide-open eye. They don't think about the divine; they just keep moving, somewhat embarrassed, walking back and forth, snapping pictures, whispering to each other.

Nearby, on the left, if you stand before the ancient façade, you'll see Little Girl Grandma's Home.

One morning, Grandma takes Sister and I there, so they can see the Home from the outside. They take the bus and have to walk a bit.

But first they pass through the portico and step inside the circular building, and Grandma shows them the great emptiness within. They push toward the middle of the temple: a lady and two children standing in the eye.

Seen from the outside, Little Girl Grandma's Home has four rows of windows. Grandma points to the top row, beneath the cornice; the façade is a white sheet of paper where things are written that Sister and I can't decipher.

Grandma reads them aloud.

"Once upon a time there was Little Girl Grandma, and now she's gone."

"She once was rich and now she owns almost nothing."

"She could live on the fifth floor and not underground like a rat."

Shortly after, they wait at their stop for the bus to take them back to the Underground Home, on the hill. If there's time, first they'll see the cannon that fires on Rome.

Others wait with them, too; the group grows larger by the minute. It's a lonely tangle; nothing and no one can be discerned. At a slight distance from the group is Grandma, with Sister and I on either side: an angel with wings, though forced to walk. That's why the angel takes the bus, crowded in among the others.

Getting off the bus now, the angel's wings are crumpled and need to unfurl, before the angel sets off toward home.

57

Home Inside the Fence, 2012

The space in the Home is reduced to two points of light plus the television set. Darkness takes the rest, on this early evening of the final night of the year.

Outside are distant Christmas lights, not many: a sterile exercise, advertising, in an area where people mainly come home just to sleep. Mall decorations, mostly, compensating for—accentuating—the sad, unlit storefronts. Blinking lights that sporadically animate the darkness inside the Home Inside the Fence.

One of the two points of light is in the kitchen. Weak, only a glimmer, a trickle that won't illuminate an entire body. The light over the stove, actually, which always goes on with the hood fan. So the space is dim and noisy besides.

Standing in this light is Mother, at least her face and neck. Her head is suspended, at a tilt, while she looks down at a landscape of pans. The hood light reveals her gray roots, not visible in the mirror, a fountain of gray spouting on her skull.

Stirring, sizzling onions, the tap-tap of the knife on the cutting board: these are the only sounds. Along with Mother's sniffling, from the onions.

In the dark, beyond the rest of her body, the kitchen table is set for dinner. Two settings across from each other, stacked plates for various courses, appropriate silverware, glasses for water and wine.

Not exactly dark, though—that's exaggerating—you can see the table because of the lights outside, by the fence. It's prison light, practically shadowless: white, overbearing, dense, pushing on the six reinforced-concrete cubes. Which means, no matter how much time a person spends on decorating, no matter how much effort is put into removing the inside from the domineering concrete out-side—attention to rugs, furniture, lighting—those outside lights always draw you back to the fence.

Now this light is spilling onto the newly set table, the double plates, the red tablecloth, the candle that will remain unlit. Mother doesn't notice, just keeps working on the finishing touches; she doesn't bother to look outside anymore.

The second point of light comes from the dining room adjacent to the kitchen: a floor lamp next to the couch. It casts a soft glow, but the lightbulb is too large for the lamp and spoils the effect.

In front of the couch, the TV is on; the remote lies abandoned on the cushions, which still bear the imprint where Father was sit-ting. On the screen, in the semidarkness, a flashing electric solilo-quy: a Hollywood-style holiday classic, and then the occasional ad for cars, sparkling wine, anti-anxiety meds, antacid tablets. All of it at a very high volume, given that no one's there to listen.

Past this space, in Sister and I's former room—now stripped of its furniture, turned into a den—Father's face is all that appears in the darkness, cut off by the computer monitor, a yawning mouth of light. The scene revolves around Mother calling him; Father is lost in what he's viewing, typing away, eyes on the screen, a thousand years away from everything around him. Mother's cooking is background noise that can't scratch the digital absence Father has settled into.

The rest of the Home Inside the Fence, this evening, especially right now, doesn't really count. Shadows are spreading—the bathroom and closet are completely dark—over the bed.

Close to the couch: the round table for entertaining dinner guests. Fallen into disuse, a lonely thing begging for handouts of light from the other two rooms, but mainly left to the dark.

(Soon, it will be time for dinner; Mother will try to pull Father away from the computer screen; he won't hear her; the dishes will sit alone, steaming away in the kitchen, waiting. Mother will try again as the dishes stop steaming; she'll sit down in his indentation in front of the TV. Then Father will come in, turn off the TV. He'll enter the kitchen, sit down at his place. Mother, after reheating the antipasto, will stand beside him. Then she'll sit down, too, and start eating, silently, before the silence of her husband. The fountain of gray hair will continue to sprout on her head until midnight, when they'll turn on the small TV in the kitchen, to watch the countdown along with the television audience.

This year, too, Mother will suggest they try calling I to wish him a happy new year and find out how he's doing, and Father won't answer. And this time, too, there will be a recorded voice saying the number's no longer in service. They'll leave him a message anyway that crashes into the wall of a changed number. Soon after, Father will grab the phone, remove his glasses, and send I an insulting text, cursing at him. Mother will write something to Sister—they'll probably get her formal "Thank you" the following day. They'll receive the usual "Happy New Year" from Relatives, that Mother will read out loud to Father, and Father won't hear; Mother will answer something back, though who knows what.

They'll go to bed before one; the bedroom's rolling shutters will block the light from the street. But the shutters will stay up in the other rooms; the lamps outside will throw their melancholy over the nighttime Home Inside the Fence. The cellphone, still on, will sit on the table.

They'll try again the following year.)

58

Underground Home, 2005

Four hundred meters from the Underground Home is a pond. You get to it down a street through the old working-class neighborhoods, which have changed some, not entirely, but all shifting with similar intent, toward the respectable.

There's a gate to a villa before reaching this pond. It opens early in the morning; sometimes a couple is standing out there, or groups of runners in shorts who jump in place, with earbuds in their ears. Once the gate opens, the groups disband: they're actually individual employees, their running gear purchased in specialty shops; if they work out first—they all discovered this—they feel better about heading to the office afterward. Jogging is good for capital.

At that time of the morning, you'll also find drowsy men and their dogs. The men have come to understand: if the dog gets to run, it won't eat the couch. The men listlessly toss sticks and stones, and the dogs joyfully fetch them back, while the men phone their lovers, if they have them, or else their mothers.

Down the dirt road past the gate, you walk under an arcade of leaves from the trees bowing over this space. Two turns, and you reach the pond.

About twenty years back, nutria swam here, almost entirely

submerged, like alligators, only a bit of fur visible, the rest of their rat length below the surface.

Behind them, the water seemed to zipper open.

The nutria would flash their orange teeth at children. And the children, armed by their fathers and mothers, would hurl bread.

Now the nutria seem to have disappeared. The water is smooth, only rippling with a strong breeze.

Along the path around the pond, about every ten meters, is a bench with a rickety wood railing in front. The children lean over this rail, and they wave frantically, throw crusts of bread at the water, as well as the cookies their mothers give them.

Down below, in the water but close to the bank, small faces—almost human, but sculpted—are showing.

About a dozen turtles sun themselves and shift about, in the presence of the human beings calling from above. The sun strikes their mosaic shells, their remote, ancient homes.

They're the castoffs of children who once wanted them, and then grew bored. The children, after watching the turtles wander around their home or swimming awkwardly in an aquarium, decided they'd had their fill. When they first got them, the turtles were about the size of walnuts, and then one day they were giants, prehistory shuffling around in armor.

So the pond took them in, replacing the nutria rats. Usually, the children's mothers abandon the turtles there, a sort of rite of deliverance: the mothers come in the evening and surrender them to the surrogate primordial broth.

When they see the families by the rail, the children with their food ammunition, the turtles push and clamber over each other toward the bank. Not out of hunger, or for attention. It's a mute protest, instead, of the species.

59

Family's Elegant Home, 2019

The Elegant Home has returned to pure space; it coincides with the floor plan in the land registry files. So it's only brick surfaces now and flooring, and the echo's been let loose, has returned since it was first shown the door at the arrival of I's furniture alongside Wife's and Little Girl's.

Now this echo, released, wanders through the empty Home. It came back in when the last piece of furniture went out, squeezed past the door: I's blue wardrobe, dismantled to its components, set on end, side by side, cabinet doors taped. The echo slipped in before the front door was locked on all that emptiness.

So initially the echo spread the thump of the knocker, the closing of the door, and the click of the lock.

Now the echo spreads the sound of a portable radio, and voices. All somewhat muffled, yet amplified, too. The radio sits on the floor; it sprays music and a low buzz of words. The echo takes these, disperses them through the apartment. The open windows don't disturb its work.

The voices are foreign, mainly Slavic, perhaps, but not just Slavic, there's a Latino counterpoint as well. And then the voices might be just one voice that becomes a chorus with the radio. Sometimes the singing is interrupted by a cough, and then resumes.

The echo faithfully reproduces it all.

To complete the Home's score: the addition of a soft, regular beat. The timbre is unmistakable, the paintbrush against the wall, the percussion of bristles, the liquid sneer—at every touch—of paint on brick.

There's another regular, though infrequent, beat: the color bucket against the wood floor, lifted, moved someplace else, first by a hand, then—somewhat fussily—by the echo.

If a smell were added, it would be the strong scent of chemical clean, the hygienics of execution: all the chaff of previous life, all the Home's remaining voice fragments clinging to the dust on the walls, must be suffocated: beaten and tugged, struck with a paintbrush, drowned in this glue, everything that moves, even if invisible.

Only with this white death is there resurrection, false resurrection. Because life is always life: it's just life below.

60

Friendship Home, 2017

A ROOM ONLY A FEW square meters in size, already prepared for the night. The light, mainly from streetlamps outside, blots out the darkness. The silence is that of a humming generator—belonging to a pizzeria—in the building's interior courtyard.

Sheets of white paper cover the bedroom walls. Crayon drawings, pink crayon mainly. There's an evolution in style and subject matter—the most recent show talent. Drawing after drawing— even the alphabet has been domesticated—the final drawings are of letters that compose a name and display beginning awareness of a signature.

There's a small table, a chair tucked beneath. On the table are sheets of A4 paper, markers, and colored pencils. And then a bed and nightstand against the wall, to the right of the door. A little girl's bed, small, white wood frame, protective siderail. A cream-colored bedspread with a firmament of pink fairies in tiaras. The fairies scatter tiny stars across the bed, the comforter, enveloped in a starry spell.

In this bed, lies I, all six two of him, according to his ID.

He's in the fetal position, legs scrunched to stay within the frame. Head resting on a pair of fairies on the pillow, and stardust sprinkled in his hair.

His eyes are open. He stares at the siderail. On the floor, an open suitcase—a carry-on. He looks down, into it: an isolated home in the night, a polypropylene building, door raised. He can make out shirt collars, rolled-up socks, his passport, deodorant stick, a pair of flip-flops held together by a rubber band. And a yellow folder—with Wife's delicate handwriting on it, in felt-tip, "Documents, I."

A small Plexiglas heart, sitting on a shelf, radiates a soft, reassuring pink glow, not as bright as the streetlights. The heart goes on automatically with the dark: I noticed the heart when he clicked off the bedside lamp, but just left it. He regrets this now.

The rest of the Home is immersed in darkness. It's an apartment I knows well, has visited many times. He showed up at 9:30 that night, after a day spent dragging his suitcase around and wondering what to do, after leaving Family's Elegant Home at dawn, and forever. Finally, he pushed the downstairs buzzer; they met him at their door: two adults and a little girl, I's longtime friends. No need to say anything, just distract the girl so she didn't fully understand what had happened.

Now the family's together in the master bedroom: father, mother, and the child, settled in again between her parents after having been kicked out the year before. She left I a book of fairies, the same fairies on her bedspread—so he could sleep better. She made it very clear, though, that this wasn't a gift: it was just for the night, and she wanted it back in the morning.

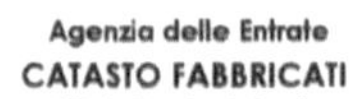

Dichiarazione protocollo n. ______ del 2 3 OTT. 2015
Planimetria di u.i.u. in Comune di ______
Via ______ civ. ______

Identificativi Catastali:
Sezione: ______
Foglio: ______
Particella: ______
Subalterno: ______

Compilata da:
______
Iscritto all'albo:
Geometri
Prov. ______   N. ______

Scheda n. 1   Scala 1:200

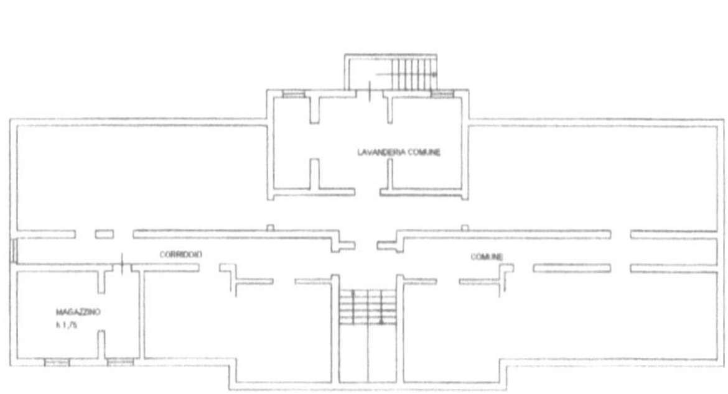

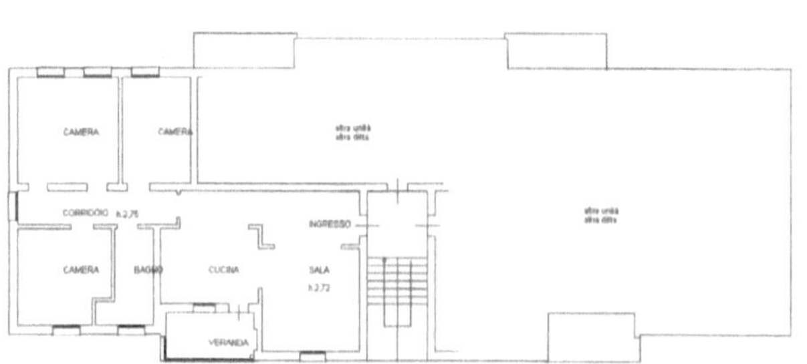

61

Home of Poet's Death, 2010

It's the view from the garden, the view from Poet's Death, facing away from the cement tree.

You can barely hear the waves hitting the shoreline of Idroscalo.

Theoretically, with it so late, there's no going in. And a sign does show the regular hours: 9:00–5:00. But you can get in any time, day or night, just by pressing the spring latch button, then unhooking the chain, and pushing open the gate.

From inside, you can see, in order: the road, the patched asphalt, the makeshift buildings, the impasto of sheet metal, brick, lime, graffiti on the walls, drawings of pricks, championships, already faded, the coupling of swastikas and various loves, all scrawled in red.

What you can't see from inside here: the labyrinth of buildings, the Idroscalo maze, three hundred meters away. The streets of this labyrinth, ending at the Tiber—the mouth of the river—are mainly dirt roads: the former asphalt has been defeated by the present. As with any labyrinth, the impression here is of many streets, though really there's only one. To muddy the waters further, this street adopts different names. It's usually Via degli Aliscafi but is sometimes also Via della Carlinga or Via dei Bastimenti.

The labyrinth takes its shape from the low buildings. Houses just thrown up—fifty years of improvising: boxes welded to other existing boxes, raised by trial and error, with street smarts, risk-taking, a lot of mistakes, and an instinct for survival.

Not shacks—to call them "shacks" is to misunderstand their intention. First built in the '60s, they're of their time: construction as the resurrection in brick of a country, with small apartment buildings, balconies all the same, awnings.

If elsewhere this was all vertical, in Idroscalo, it stopped at two stories. No construction firms at work: just bare hands and inexperience. The dream, however, was still the same, still middle-class, of being the protagonist in creating your own home. But, no, not shacks—modeled after beach houses: semidetached, cobbled-together cottages rising, one after the other, side-by-side, none of them alike. A small (shabby) yard, a parking pad.

The labyrinth consists of fifty independent structures, according to the most recent census, where fifty-three families live, seventeen with underage children. One hundred and fifty-three people total—which means, however, that some escaped the cage of identification. Ninety-four identified, ninety-eight residents, fifty-five nonresidents. Also cited, registered: thirty-six dogs, nine cats, and one horse.

With your back to Poet's Death, you can see a State armored vehicle, barred windows, riot-ready, going down Via dell'Idroscalo. Then another of these police vehicles, then three Carabinieri jeeps. Army bringing up the rear. Rumbling down the road, tires and engines. And added to all this, a helicopter, blades whirring over the labyrinth, cutting through the fog, the shock of it, this strange, motorized insect.

Meanwhile, Poet's Death remains asleep; this is a dream, a reworking of the past, bolus. The spider's web spreads over the cement tree, a different geometric structure from the jeeps, but with the same aim, the surprise assault. No sign of the turtle; she might be in brumation.

Finally, slowly, come the heavy construction vehicles. A parade of excavators, tracks steadily pounding the ground. Clumsy, mechanized dinosaurs, pachyderms with an instinct for destruction. Their heads held high on long necks, ready to strike, to smash through surfaces with their snouts. Yellow, clumsy bullies, they roll on, toward the labyrinth.

The parade is over now, with only a rumbling trail; the view, from behind the bars, as always: Oriflex, Mattress and Boxspring Factory, 06-568-0431.

Soon after, screaming explodes in the distance: men and women, arms raised against the mechanized dinosaurs and their digging, against the soldiers with their helmets and shields. Mostly women, defending their dwellings with their bodies, facing these others, staking a different claim from that of the State, the idea that every human has the right to a home.

From inside the cage, you can see the parade going by in reverse. First, the same as before, and last the pachyderms, jaws now stained with concrete. But this, this is only a raid, demolition just for show, a first warning in the unequal struggle for dignity—an army against a few poor folk. The drivers look weary from a hard day's work, but their eyes flash satisfaction.

Poet's Death is what remains in the background, when all the rest is quiet. The night, now fallen over Idroscalo, gives back the sea. At times the gate creaks, is heard even in the labyrinth, but no one pays it any mind. Just the sound of those coming and going, in search of a little peace, away from the streetlights. Someone leans back against the cement tree, scrambles to his feet soon after; other times, someone remains slouched there, overdosing, and is carried off the next day. Afterwards, once again, there's little left—a fierce elegy, the ordinary liturgy of decay.

62

Home of the State, 1997

IT'S AT NIGHT, MAINLY, WHEN a lack of meaning takes over, when I startles at the slightest sound, an echo amplifying the nothingness inside this empty building. An immense nothingness, and I is embedded here, in a room of a few square meters, in a place that can only lay claim to a record of failure, first—remember—as a town hall, then a school, then an empty space with no real purpose, an expenditure for the council to justify, a local controversy, always on the verge of being put up for auction.

Sometimes the night is never-ending, and winter drags on; twelve months, now reduced to ten, I's debt to the State as a male entering the world, but it feels like this night is eternal. Buried under layers of blankets in an ex-janitor's closet, in a marginal corner of a deserted building, a TV on a chair like a consolation prize, three morning buses from here to where he does his service, all day in front of a flashing Xerox machine: that's his payment to avoid the single night train back to the Home Inside the Fence.

For I, though, the janitor's closet is a source of comfort, a vestige of school, though I barely remembers anything from his time in school, perhaps just a sort of torpor, a tepid clamminess, the hatching of an equation, or something in Latin. That's why I is basically happy here, even when he loses the overall sense of things. The alarm clock—not the bell—will bring him back to the world in the morning, and he'll be lying in a landscape already defined by memory. To fall asleep, he writes poems in a notebook, which he'll leave under the bed, along with his glasses and cellphone. Then, if he can't sleep, if the lack of meaning prevails, he masturbates, and the hot, thick semen overwhelms the feverish workings of his brain, a tabula rasa, leading straight to dreams.

Other times, like now, he leaves his room. He walks around outside the building with his hands in his pockets, his shoulders hunched if it's cold, if he's in a good mood, a cigarette or a stick of gum. What he sees: cars parked below streetlights. Otherwise, potholes and patched asphalt, the daily axle war.

This is his first time into the park, though there's not much to see at night. The place's fame precedes it: in the middle of the park stands an immense building, the old abandoned asylum: the doors finally opened, perhaps in the late '70s, I doesn't remember—but he has seen this building before, it's in his gray matter—the May newspaper containing both the body of murdered Prisoner and all the freed lunatics of Italy.

At four in the morning, the building is like a sinkhole; I walks past, not thinking of anything, except that he can't sleep. In three hours, it will be dawn. He skirts that monument to the fissure in the psyche, with only a trail of smoke behind him, and his clouded breath before him. The snow in the field is a bruised, shining blue beneath the full disc of the moon. The bare trees wait patiently for spring. The puddles have an icy film, and I instinctively avoids them.

Not much to say, except that I considers himself happy, in this special solitude. He pulls his wool cap down over his ears, watches his own shadow, to the side, escorting him out of the park. He knows that before long, the electric coffee pot will snap him awake, like the cold couldn't. He'll pull the covers back up over the bed, like a grown man. Then he'll write a few more lines in his notebook, and feel he's a poet.

(He won't see, as he leaves the park, that small section of the asylum where the lights stay on every night, that handful of windows behind bars. He walked past and didn't turn his head. No, he probably did see, but he wasn't paying attention, so perhaps he'll remember, all of a sudden, one night in the future, and he'll wonder about those windows. He was wearing headphones—some rock lullaby, guitar, vocals—so didn't hear the screams erupting from the park.

He didn't see the two faces watching him go by from the window. Behind them, white stretchers and hospital beds, the sour smell of medications, a pair of nurses in uniform, who took these two by the arm and led them back to bed, then got each of them to sleep with a needle pushed into a vein. And so their screams—like an animal in a trap—trailed off, and the park was left to the wind on the snow.

But I was already at the front door to his building, yawning, slipping his key into the lock. The garbage men were emptying the dumpsters; the first cars were rounding the park, headed for the bypass.

In a few hours, the noise of the day would block out the

screams from that corner of the park, from those remnants of the liberation—liberated thirty years before but left in the asylum, due to a lack of relatives, so still tended to: kept alive and sedated by the State. A playground—*To safeguard the younger generation,* as it was written—was built behind the building, at a suitable distance.)

63

Family's Elegant Home, 2017

WHILE THE ELEVATOR CABIN IS transparent, it's the black box for the building of Family's Elegant Home. This period piece seems to be some kind of controller, a panoptic box sliding up and down, allowing a view of the entryway to each apartment. But really, it's a space that bares all: anyone on the stairs or leaning over the rail sees every last detail, vertically, of those going up or down: how they stand, check their cellphone, if their hair is dirty, if they dig a finger into their ear, if the dog is gnawing their shoe—the clear impatience of two human beings forced into the same square meter. Thinking they're protected by the rules of theater, by an enclosed space, the residents, only semiconscious, are completely exposed. They slide up and down the spine of an experiment.

So, a reverse panopticon: it's not the person inside checking on those in their apartments; it's those outside on the stairs who do the looking and the dominating. And this is what also reinforces the social role—central, prominent—of the building manager in the condominium organizational chart. The elevator is the tangible instrument of her power. She's the one who attends to its maintenance; she's the one who alerts the proper contractor; she's the one who stays on the ground floor or somewhere on the stairs and talks to the technicians working on the elevator stuck between floors. She looms over them, imperious, while they lean down to check the relays, and stand there in their safety work boots, suspended in the void, balancing on the back of an animal—its organs, a motor and a counterweight—that refuses to fly.

And it's no accident, either, that the building manager is in charge of cleaning the elevator cabin. She does this weekly, just like the stairs. Naturally, she concentrates on the glass, so eighty percent of the elevator (the rest of it is fine wood). The glass must be cleaned—there can be no impediment to the view of what's going on inside. Perhaps this is an instrument of class revenge, the domination of the subordinate class over the *signori*, but it is only this salaried eye which reports that all is in functioning order.

And indeed, this elevator cabin, now making its controlled climb, contains—expressed in breath, in molecules, in silence—every last detail of what led to the ending of a love. Over the years, it saw I go up alone, with Wife, or packed in with Family. Saw them talking, surrounded by their groceries; leaned up against the glass; angry, teeth clenched; or else instinctively holding hands. Saw Wife run her fingers through I's hair after a storm; Little Girl plop down on the floor; the three of them introducing themselves to others without handshakes, due to limited space. Saw Little Girl and I chattering away at the beginning, then less and less. Saw the three of them always together at first, then more and more of I on his own, going down, and Wife alone with Little Girl again. Once, late at night, it saw I going down with a pillow, and a door slamming behind him, then I going back up the following day, in broad daylight, with the pillow stuffed into a bag.

The elevator's the one that knows more than anyone else about why a love ends, why it's over in an instant, what has happened, why a branch breaks, and a family suddenly falls. It knows the secret, even if it doesn't know how to say it, has no words to say it, only many layers built up over time. But it might be looking for this secret now, in the wormholes in the wood, now that the cabin is on the ground floor again, and throwing its light onto the lobby, into the dense, five o'clock darkness. One minute after I came down with his roller bag, in the dark early morning, a knot in his throat, the cables and winding drum slowing his descent, preventing his fall. One minute after I, headed down to the lobby, met the counterweight at the halfway point, rising up, in his place.

64

Underground Home/Sea Branch, 1992

STILL A GENERAL PICTURE OF vacationing. Meaning: a fictional life, life with work expunged. Or: a more simplified version of life for humans, without the brain's groundless fears. (The instructions are simple: lock up the Home where the tax notices come, and move someplace different, like the other but devitalized, a place with no surprises, where the State can't get in, where no one calls; then turn yourself into individuals committed to fattening up, 20 percent movie stars, 80 percent retirees.)

The scene brought about with people at their railings, people in colored tank tops or else shirtless, or in bikinis, practically purple those first days, then tanned—smoke rising from burning charcoal and then the smell of barbecue. The balconies here, in this particular case, overlook the garden of the Underground Home/Summer Branch, Grandma's pride and debt, already described on previous pages, this, also a fictional life, sometimes belonging to the summer thriller genre: screams in the night, dangerous objects at ground zero, Father attempting and failing to hack up a polycarbonate canoe with a kitchen cleaver, then shoving the blade in I's face, the teenager not reacting, but terrified—with Grandma a tragic chorus, howling, "Stop it!," reeling, hands raised, and Mother not saying anything, like usual, her automatic crying, just letting it all happen, offering her son as a sacrifice to her husband, so Father will still love her—or Father hitting I in the face, over and over, with his fist, even with a one-two sucker punch, a macho revival of his youth, pinning I down, knees on his arms, I lying on the lawn not sure of what's going on, and a neighbor's voice—a solitary chorus member on a balcony: "Leave him alone, he's just a kid!" While three hundred meters in the distance, the sea keeps on with its lazy to-and-fro of sunset shells and foam.

Put another way: those balconies and terraces are a set of boxes—the surrounding buildings are mainly three-stories—and from their galleries, the vacationers attend the theater. With amusement, early on, then with annoyance, because they paid for a different show. So, the complaints to the owner—this isn't what they signed up for—and hanging out on the balcony less and less, their back to the rail, muttered comments, a quick cigarette or two.

But there's also relief—unexpected, unhoped-for, and therefore more regenerative—and sometimes a sense of vacation is restored to the vacationers overlooking the garden. As is happening now and has happened several times before: Father is loading up the car before the end of summer, arranging the suitcases in the trunk with geometric rancor, then leaving, barely saying goodbye.

All this usually happens early in the morning. A few hours later, Grandma appears in the garden. She sits, staring, exhausted and defeated, in bruised peace. Which is still a better show from the balconies: the silence before the final curtain. Then comes September, like every other year.

65

Home of the Gasometro, 2020

THE TABLE IS THE MAIN piece of furniture. It's in the kitchen. And the rest of the room rotates around its axis; to some extent, you're obliged to stay seated. A rug and an armchair, fairly close, give credence to the term, "living room."

From the table, what you see out the two windows is Rome. Narrowing in, closer to home: the mild Sabine hills, Aventine Hill, the Tiber, and then the small building, a pure expression of the 1970s building industry, the optimization of space, volume divided into lodgings. On the right, the gridiron monument of the Gasometro, the new industrial Colosseum. Worn out, defunct, eaten away by rust (hence, its color), the Gasometro makes for a good photo: a dead body that won't spoil the view. The new symbol of Rome.

To its left, not really visible, other examples of this same species: three small gasometri, only one surviving, functioning, and ignored like the others. And you can't make out the flame at its center. The flame that's closer, right now, is the pale blue flame of a burner, behind I, so behind the table. Over this flame sits a modest-sized, gurgling caffettiera. Then this flame goes out.

The rest of the apartment is only one other room, door closed. The two rooms are joined by a paved, narrow lane.

I is sitting with his laptop open, his hands on the keys, and nearby is an espresso cup, a glass, and a carafe of water. The espresso cup, the glass, the carafe, the table, the chair, none of these are his: the Home of the Gasometro is a furnished apartment.

On the ring finger of his left hand: the furrow of his wedding ring, disappearing, just corporeal memory now.

For the first time, I is testing out the thrill of owning nothing; the ballast of his furniture has been abandoned to its fate. The Home of the Gasometro, then, is only a backdrop. With the ballast of his possession left on the ground, I flew: the apartment is on the ninth floor, the final floor before the sky—and is sky already to anyone looking up from the street.

On his terrace, gulls catch their breath, then hurl themselves off the building.

Over the past weeks, opening the window, closing it, makes little difference. I tries something now and then; he opens the window and door to the balcony, eliminating the division between outside and inside. But it's the same silence on the balcony: the outside is like the inside, minus the hum of the refrigerator in the kitchen, a relief from the quiet. But outside, that quiet is a scared panorama, Rome, a seemingly frozen image; the streets are streets and they're empty, the buildings are solidified space, the silence is in reinforced concrete—except for the wind, a slight hiss, in every corner.

So Rome is still Rome, but with no bodies on the streets, it makes for perfect photos from the balconies, where the citizens have barricaded themselves. Except no one wants to take these pictures; with no people, beauty is frightening, reveals its invented, commercial nature, its link to capitalism: with nothing to sell, there's not much to see. Even spring is painful: the faces on the balconies are grimaces, lips pressed tight; there's something sordid to the flowers, sexual organs yawning open, exposed; the sky is blue, but a pointless blue: the physical nature of this color has cauterized emotion.

So I prefers to stay inside. When he opens the window in the morning, it's just a habit. He always looks out at the Gasometro, the chain of hills, but he doesn't really see them, has stopped purposefully trying to see. He opens the window, almost to mortify hope. But then the wisteria assails him; his sense of smell bores through even this most miserable of prophesies, is swollen with life already lived, with remembrance: it offers him an ideal past, stripped of bitterness, a life that could be called life.

I looks at the white blooms, goes out to the balcony, gets the hose and starts watering the flowers because it's a part of the lease agreement between landlord and tenant, rent lowered for plant care—a clear pact that exonerates him from the humiliation of talking to the plants, from being overly sentimental. Watering every other day in April, every day when the temperature rises, and this means summer, if, according to the papers, people go back to going out. If, that is, people go back to dying from a variety of things, not just the one thing that's killing them, this year's official cause of death, death by proximity.

Back at the kitchen table, I stares at his screen and doesn't type, his fingers hovering over the keys, ready to strike, a quick motion, a percussive motion. All that's clear is that he's writing with the end in mind.

Gulls skim the balcony, searching for the sea, a forgivable error in perception: they should keep going about another ten kilometers, but they don't; beaks thrown open against the top of the buildings, they swoop down on the black bags left beside the dumpsters—the only action granted by Decree, taking in a breath of air along with the garbage, looking at Rome beside scraps, then decay, in the early heat.

Under the floor, in the apartment below, come two voices. A vibration underfoot. One is a baby's voice. The other, a woman's. These two are part of the stereo sound of these many weeks, the sealed-in families, the exhausted, vibrating vocal cords of an entire apartment building.

I shuts his laptop and rubs his eyes as if he's just rousing from a long sleep. Unfinished, inside, a line he just wrote: "He thinks life is a beautiful place, even so." He'll probably wind up deleting this, when he goes back to it.

The baby's voice from downstairs is a constant beat: a steady "I" without pause, drawn out to two syllables: "I-ye," "I-ye," "I-ye." Added to this is the woman's voice, saying "you." I, at the laptop again, writes "I," distractedly, as if taking dictation. He hears the baby running and screaming his personal pronoun. I gets up, goes to the window, raps on the glass, tries to catch a gull's attention. If the bird looks at him, he'll point toward the sea, down by Fiumicino— it's stopped too soon.

66

Red Home on Wheels, 1978

THE HATCH IS OPEN; PRISONER's body lies curled up in nice clothes. And into this small metal space comes I on all fours. The tunnel is what joins the TV's rectangle of light in the Underground Home to this sheet-metal space in the Renault 4.

And that's how I crossed Rome, immersed in dazzling lava, propelled by incandescent waves, and suddenly washed up inside the Red Home on Wheels. Once there, he crawled around in his diaper, saw every centimeter of Prisoner's body, up close: the closed eyes, the knotted tie.

He saw how this final Home was made, the rear seat, the windows, the lit dome light, the doors open, the street; he certainly saw the astonished faces looking in.

Someone, leaning forward, perhaps saw I; someone else saw the TV's rectangle of light appear in his own home. Most of them, though, didn't notice a thing. Just as they didn't notice the stream of light carrying away the nation's children.

There was too much noise: sirens, screaming, the helicopter tearing up the looming sky.

Even though he was right there, I heard nothing. He didn't

hear the water in the fountain, fifty meters from the Red Home on Wheels. It would only have taken a few baby steps for him to see it.

The fountain stands in the middle of the piazza and includes ephebes, amphorae, and dolphins. On top are four turtles, freed from the water, taking flight, reaching for the sky between the buildings.

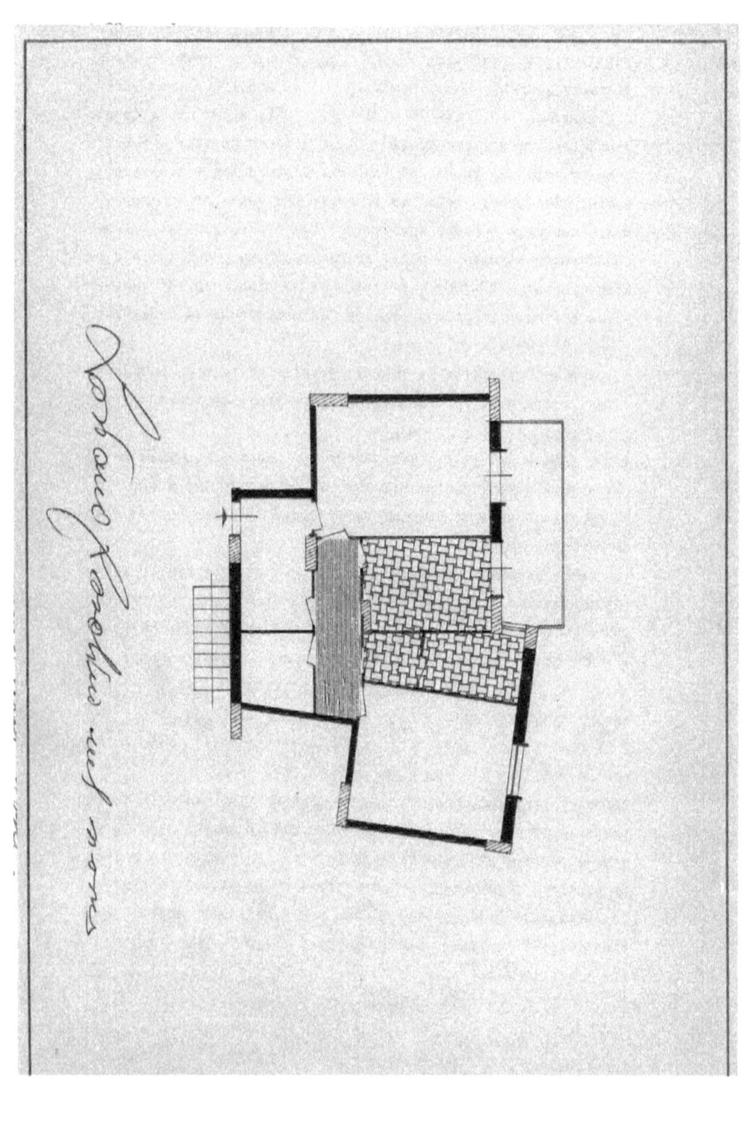

67

Underground Home, 1975

ONE OF I'S FIRST MEMORIES is Sister's face. It's blurry, doesn't come to him at once. The start of this memory is vague, is mostly smells, his first experience of things, a sensory tangle. And shadows: the world is a single, deformed mass against white; the light is a net into which I has fallen.

Falling into the world, I has begun to pluck every shadow from the tree of light he's found; every day, he's dropped more shadows into his bag of things, where they're forgotten.

But he hasn't forgotten Sister's face when he first entered the Home.

Not exactly a face, more a scream from the middle of the floor when she sees I for the first time. I is only a warm bundle, yet he's what blows up Sister's kingdom: this wasn't expected, that in her contract with life, the world wasn't hers alone.

I is Sister's deepest fear; and like all fears, it originates deep within the species. In an instant, it climbs back up millions of years and cerebral cortexes, scales bones, slips into veins, then bursts like water from a rock into the present, appearing inside the last dilated pupil.

The apocalypse, for Sister, is in the guise of an almost blind newborn.

231

68

Home of Adultery/Branch Office, 1995

THE HOME HAS A REMOTE branch office, far from the city center. Out in the country, though officially, it doesn't exist. It's in the land registry filed under secrets, properties not traceable to contracts, money exchanged under the table, anonymous.

Still provincial, so where everything almost blends together.

Anyone driving by will see a college-age kid—I—go inside, and the Woman with the Wedding Ring park her car out front and after a few hours, disappear again into the landscape, but this doesn't change the nonexistent nature of the Home.

The Branch Office to the Home of Adultery is in fact a key hidden under a rock, almost cubelike, though not orthogonal—the rock is gently rounded, due to erosion. It sits on a low, dry stone wall, so doesn't seem particularly out of place. If you lift this rock, you'll find the key and can go in.

The key, then, is what makes the Home exist for I and the Woman with the Wedding Ring. The first to arrive opens the door, and the other just steps inside. Once the door is closed, the Home's precise physiology is set in motion. In here, the two laugh, cry, and make love.

The fact that it's not on any detailed maps—for Husband of Woman with the Wedding Ring and for Father and Mother—of course doesn't mean the Home isn't located somewhere, but it's located on a map of secrets. I is inside the Home, but for Mother and Father, he's in a university lecture hall, doing what he's supposed to be doing; for Husband, Woman with the Wedding Ring is on a large grocery run—the weekly shopping, a packed car, savings.

The Branch Office to the Home of Adultery is mainly a fictional space: it's where I, age twenty, gets to play grown-up.

His access to this Home is through love. It would be a mistake to interpret the sex here as just a performance of gonads and endorphins, a youthful diving into the body of a married woman. This isn't what drives I in this covert relationship, and it's probably not what drives the woman to break the rules of faith and family.

Actually, the Branch Office is evidence to the contrary: for I, it's the perfect backdrop for testing out adult life—a stereotypical, bourgeois adult life—during his college years. Creating a family, a home to take care of, wood to chop, a dry wall to maintain, a little restoration work, a little masonry, tackling water damage, dampness, fixing the gutter so water drains into the communal drainage system. Rather shoddy work, of course, but still functional in the short term, or for a bit longer, to maintain the fiction of being the perfect husband, a model of efficiency.

In this fiction, in this theater of uneven, willy-nilly stones, Woman with the Wedding Ring plays her role as the wife—she does have some credentials for this, after all, considering her name in State and Church records. When she arrives, she opens the door and knows how to arrange the various details of a home. In fact, she comes in as a wife and she stays one—just a revised version—a half hour of imagining how life would be, if only it weren't.

There's certainly a fair amount of sex, and the assaults of a twenty-year-old (from Woman with the Wedding Ring's perspective) or the art of well-seasoned love (from I's perspective) must play a part. But it's the "after-love" that really counts, the performance of family, making room in the fridge, the dish soap, deciding where the bench should go, sitting and talking: about a future together they both take for granted, though there won't be any future together.

The ending's always the same: the closed door, the key under the rock. The Home goes back to being a dump out in the country that doesn't warrant a description and doesn't want one, for the sake of privacy.

I gets into Woman with the Wedding Ring's car—driver's side—the usual ending, to maintain the fiction until the last possible moment, and he drives along this country road with her sitting beside him, rummaging through her official life in her purse. Before they reach the turnoff, he pulls to the side of the road and gets out, and Woman with the Wedding Ring slides over, behind the wheel. I takes his travel bag out from the back and quietly says goodbye.

There's next to nothing after this—it's the end of the show. There's a college kid walking along a country road with a lumpy travel bag. He turns, walks backwards a few steps, thumb out. Sometimes he's successful and runs to a car waiting up ahead, window down, blinker on; he jumps in, pulls off a few kid lines, gets out at the station, raising his thumb again in thanks.

The Branch Office to the Home of Adultery stays as is; there's not much to say and the locals say it: a few wisecracks when they see the two leave, less even—a knowing, tired look, again, but thinking about other things. Show's over, folks—hard to say when it'll be back.

69

Home of the Return to Adolescence, 2014

IF THE CONTEXT, THE PEOPLE, the spatial arrangement of the bodies are what make a place a home, then we would be in the Underground Home/Sea Branch. That is, where bamboo fencing divides the world into classes, and I stands by this division, then steps over the threshold, soccer ball under his arm, the swim resort behind him, and ahead, past the partition, the straightforward appeal of the locals, some of them playing soccer with I in the late afternoon, then leaving afterward. And nearby, the gentle, steady lapping of the Tyrrhenian Sea.

Except this boy—I only knows him by his nickname—is now bald with a grizzled goatee, and what divides them is the front desk of a London hotel. A hotel that has rugs by the front desk and pictures on the walls, a moderately luxurious hotel, with tasteful lighting. So a hotel like many—the British version. Concerning the boy, there's still that eagle on his neck—I remembers the eagle—but now it soars in a very different sky: a wing poking out from a white shirt beneath a suit. And rounding out the picture, oval glasses, out of style for a few years, and a subdued quality that seems a bit like worn-down rage.

A nametag on his chest, finally, and a name I doesn't recognize. And he wouldn't have recognized him at all, if the other hadn't made himself known, after a brief pantomime, that is, first registering his passport, answering I in English, saying there was a fax from the Embassy, everything was covered, welcome to London, here's a city map, feel free to call down to the front desk at any time—and then suddenly, with a laugh that peels away all corporate pomposity, "*Sto fijo de 'na mignotta!*"—well, I'll be a sonofabitch—repeated three times—staring at I in disbelief.

That it's London out there, that it's nighttime, doesn't matter—everything dissolves into that comment, into discomfort—I's not sure what to do, if he should walk around behind the desk, or wait—finally, a hug, both of them, leaned over the counter, and I's promise to come down and chat before hitting the sack. Then his roller bag in the elevator, his room on the fourth floor, a tip for the Senegal bellboy. And that discomfort, lying on the bed, feeling helpless, exposed, the exact opposite of the flawless protection provided by hotels—they're supposed to be embassies, luxurious sanctuaries that sanitize you from yourself.

I tries showering, then lies down again in his towel: he looks at the map, distracted. It stings, this bitter feeling, this scrutiny from his own adolescence, so opposite to the natural flow of things. Life, out of whack, watches him from below, from the lobby, with no escaping into the version of himself that's been fine-tuned, unwitnessed, over time.

Now on to what happens that night: I, behind the counter, the chair the Eagle slid back there for him, the occasional slap on his shoulder, emphasizing how surprised the Eagle is to see him. And showing him the schedule of hotel arrivals and departures—a color-blocked chart—explaining to him, tie loosened, with a certain dignity, the promotions, the praise from his boss, and then about women, not much to say there, just like back then, between him and his brother, he's the one they just wanted to be friends with.

And then the sudden descent into provincial hell, what you don't see on the coast: the drug racket, the garage controlled by the mob, repairs paid with pills or with baggies, and his brother—the handsome one, who'd practically screw a shopping bag—found in his car in the family garage, face gray, a hose from the muffler to the window, and a note on the dashboard: "It's all Dad's fault," and then, misspelled: "Live is shit." Carrying that note around in his pocket for months, not knowing what to do with it, not able to show it to his parents, but tearing off the shitty life part, the more general part, that is. And his escape—it's either leave or turn out worse than them, if the note was true—and finally, England, thank god, "Getta load of this," he says, showing off his suit. "What about you?" he asks, point-blank. And I's not sure what to say, after all that, and stays quiet. Then he raises his hand, showing off his ring finger with clumsy pride: "I got married."

The Eagle smiles, says, "Good for you," and they go outside, not far from the reception desk, time enough for a quick smoke, London eaten away in the glare of the streetlight. Then an hour later, a call to someone, hotel to hotel, very late now, the voice that answers, another ex-boy, the Eagle passes the phone to I, the other voice is cheerful, speaking from an Edinburgh hotel, beyond the fence, saying, "You were always on the right side, and that's where you belonged. We've always been over here, but we're fine." The Eagle is happy, slips his phone back into his inside jacket pocket.

Then dawn finally arrives, with a glow that lets things be, but sets them back in motion. I rises from his chair, as though it's been a thousand years, his back in pieces, his eyelids swollen. Meanwhile, the morning cleaning's begun, the cleaning crew approaches the counter, the Eagle says hello, introduces I, says he's from Rome, while straightening his tie, because the boss will be there any minute. Then he says I should go get some breakfast, and I answers it's still too early. The Eagle picks up the receiver, punches in a number, then as he's talking, winks at I with a tired smile, and says in English, "*A close friend*," then hangs up. "Knock and they'll get you *da magna'*, I'm headed home soon." And when I disappears into the elevator, he puts the chair back where it was.

70

Home of the Law, 2018

THE HOME OF THE LAW is broken down by everything above it.

Yet there's still cubic volume here: to break it down is fine, but the entirety must also be kept in mind, where it fits inside the whole. The Home of the Law is one minute cell in the beehive of an austere courthouse. Seen from above, if you were to fly over Turin's city center—the Alps always in view, pointing toward the sky—the courthouse would be an immense architectural block.

A building beyond the logic of construction, not so much because of the incorporeality of the law per se (because of the level of bureaucracy and power associated with the law, meaning, the all-or-nothing paperwork involved; the arthrosis of language; the lexicon composed of printed formulas; the amphetamine effect of rulings read in monotone, in a posthuman voice), but because of the courthouse's volumetric appearance.

Its location: you could say the building is northwest of the city center, but in a way it's a seamless continuation of the center, inseparable from it, part of the metropolitan fabric, though it almost looks like an object fallen from outer space. And it's here that Family's Home relocates, in order to break apart forever.

Now insert two bodies into this space, Wife and I, standing side by side. For now, don't think about describing the interior spaces or considering the others present in the Home of the Law.

Think instead of the weight of this space where Wife and I are juxtaposed and positioned vertically. A large room: nine by twelve meters. The ceiling height: at least five meters. Now calculate the total cubature of the Home of the Law. Proceed—with engineering pedantry—by adding in the ceiling and the floor. You'll arrive at a total weight of 136,400 kilograms, or 136 tons. And it's under this weight, that Wife and I are standing. If you add their respective body weights—I's slightly underweight 82 kilograms, Wife's 53 kilograms—the change is miniscule.

In relation to all this, what's left, then—the ruling—is barely the weight of a feather. It happens without motion, in an almost empty space. To complete the picture, let's add two large windows, on the right side of the room: vertical, 2 by 1.5 meters, double-pane glass, and curtains, so what the law determines in this room will remain a secret.

Imagine three rows of chairs, plain, straight-backed, the standard sort of chair meant to disappear from memory straightaway. No one sitting on these chairs—not now—but their absence isn't felt: rather, these empty chairs are the perfect audience, what the legal machine was conceived for—the steady, bovine gaze of empty objects sitting in a row.

The last detail: a desk, the bench, parallel to the last wall. The two people seated at the bench take up a limited amount of space. But the proportions aren't what's so striking—it's their summer clothing, their suntans. The way they sit shows a clear hierarchy:

the man is relaxed and shuffles through papers, signing every-thing absentmindedly; the girl, his clerk, sits straight beside him: she points to each place where he should sign, knows what goes where.

Finally, Wife and I are there, fording the river, between the first row of chairs and the official bench. I attempts to sit down, to infuse the scene with rhetoric, but is thwarted by a wave of the hand from the gray-haired man who ratifies the law in his T-shirt: his gesture is brusque, unequivocal: Please remain standing.

Then, a tired reading, overwhelmed by the accumulated bore-dom from summer, the confirmation that I is truly I and Wife is truly Wife, with their respective tax IDs, place and date of birth, perma-nent address. The transfer of money is mentioned with no empha-sis, the amount is insubstantial in this scene, beside these windows, in this vacuum.

(More could be said about Wife and I, what they're wearing, the expressions on their faces, the gap between their arms as they stand. And about the tension pressing outwardly from their bones, which translates to annoyance, the exact opposite of intimacy. More could be said about the automatic movement of their hands, which, over the years have learned to reach for each other, but are now held in check by the brain—reminding them that what was, was, and won't return. More could be said about their defeat, about the defeat of summer.

Instead, observe their backs as they walk out of this room assigned for the confirmation of conjugal failure. See how they're watched from behind, the general indifference of the officials, their eyes vacant above the stack of files before them. Listen to their steps and to the clammy nothing of the bored state machine behind them. Observe their backs, at least within the confines of this sentence, for the time that it endures.)

71

Poet's Last Home, 1975

THERE'S NO POINT TO CONSIDERING the details of the plan, how the space is divided in Poet's Last Home. Just keep in mind—though it doesn't matter—that it's lot 105, and the plans are at a scale of 1:1000 and bound and color-coded with a 50 L stamp provided by the land registry office.

No need to describe the flow between rooms (and there are a lot of them—rooms—too many—at least nine, plus a garden), because there's just the one very small woman inside these walls, and she barely moves. The space of the living room, dining room, and kitchen would be enough. Plus the bedroom, on the other side of the apartment, and of course the bathroom.

Honestly, the living room is more than enough space, with its couch, though Poet's Mother is sitting in a chair.

Consider the following together: the minimal portion of humanized space, one's home, along with the vastness of its metropolitan context. And then: consider this living room alongside the nation.

So on the one side: flooring, walling, fixtures, furnishings—the rug, television, chairs, and tables. And on the other: small apartment buildings, potholed streets, highway interchanges, gas pumps, tree-lined avenues, old people walking their dogs, shops, well-dressed women, neighborhood decorum, overflowing garbage on the weekends. Basically—Rome: the dome of St. Peter's, the terraces, the whores along the road by the sea. Now widen the view: Italy, from Venice to the Mediterranean.

Consider the roar, the explosion of words announcing Poet's death to the world. Consider his mangled body, blown like lava ash into all the homes, onto the balconies, onto the heads of all those walking along the street. Consider Poet's death blowing over the Dome, onto eyeglasses, children's shoes, mothers' painted fingernails, train-station clocks, into ship hatches, shelters, hospital wards, onto the Mole Antonelliana, into the Strait of Messina.

Consider the newspapers, television, the pain and repetition, the gossip and rumors, the brutalized face, the sheet over the body, the indecency of this sheet not covering the shoes. After considering this, multiply it by a hundred, a thousand, to the point of retching, for all the many, the too many images and words.

Now back to the living room.

Sitting on a chair, a very small woman, a mother. She might get up, might wander around the apartment, or she might just stay put—it doesn't matter.

But the television isn't on, and there's no sign of a newspaper.

The television's not even plugged in.

But it is in the rest of the homes of the nation, brightening windows in bedrooms and dens.

Consider this action—pulling the plug—as friends might do, going to the extreme to protect someone, even if it's doomed to fail.

Consider the weight of that silence pressing down on the mother's temples; the determination in her eyes, not to know; the low roar of the nondetonation of thought: about what is false and what is true for the mind.

Consider the nothing of this, of a still-living son, when he's already dead to the rest of the world.

Mod. B (Nuovo Catasto Edilizio Urbano)

MINISTERO DELLE FINANZE
DIREZIONE GENERALE DEL CATASTO E DEI SERVIZI TECNICI ERARIALI

Lire 50

39 NUOVO CATASTO EDILIZIO URBANO
(R. DECRETO-LEGGE 13 APRILE 1939, N. 652)

Planimetria dell'immobile situato nel Comune di __________ Via __________ n. __________
Ditta __________ nato a __________ il __________ proprietario per __________
__________ nato a __________ il __________ proprietario per __________
Allegata alla dichiarazione presentata all'Ufficio Tecnico Erariale di __________

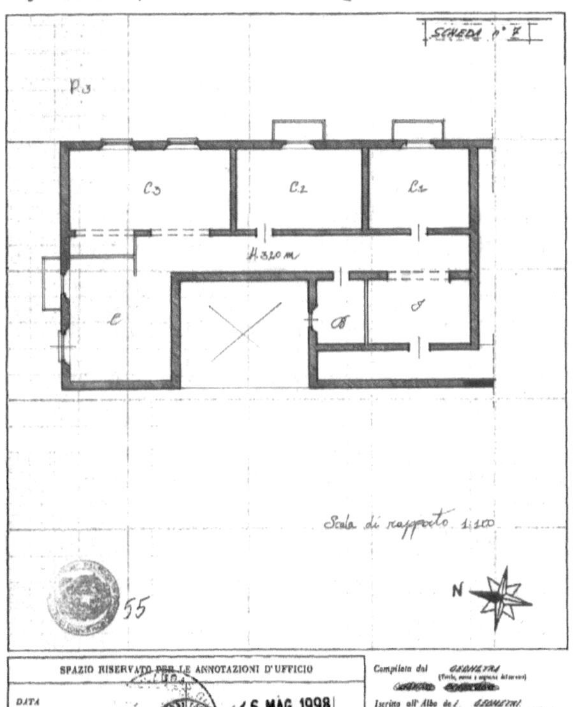

SPAZIO RISERVATO PER LE ANNOTAZIONI D'UFFICIO

DATA
PROT. N°

26 MAG. 1998

E 0079

Firma

Compilato dal GEOMETRA
(Titolo, nome e cognome del tecnico)
____
Iscritto all'Albo dei GEOMETRI
della Provincia di __________
DATA __________
Firma __________

Ultima planimetria in atti

Data presentazione __________ - Data: __________ - n. __________ - Richiedente: __________
Totale schede: I - Formato di acquisizione: A3(297x420) - Formato stampa richiesto: A4(210x297)

72

Turtle's Home, 2048

She's no longer a single unit, an independent dwelling with a yard.

Here's what happened first. Turtle received a consolation prize: I had gone, but there was lettuce. Every morning, it silently rained down from above. A meteor falling like clockwork on the neighborhood. First came the snout of a slipper or the top of a shoe; and then, always, a heel.

But this was no act of generosity—there was no feeling behind this. It was only a household chore, like turning on the lights or starting the washer. Turtle was the Triassic in the courtyard, prehistory, inherited with the Home.

Abandonment can sometimes result in a sense of victimhood or a compulsion to clean. And since Turtle isn't a sentimental reptile (as far as we know), for a very long time she sublimated I's departure by tending to her home.

And it wasn't the first time, either. A characteristic of her species is growing accustomed to extinction. She's witnessed the self-importance, the mockery of other living creatures since the Mesozoic era. Even the most overbearing of them, the ones who had the most hubris, are gone. Their tonnage, grandeur, massive rib cages, prominent teeth, erect stance with wings couldn't do for them what the existence of a home on one's back could do, in terms of preservation and survival.

From inside her carapace, looking out her window, Turtle has seen millions of the overbearing and bellicose roofless go by, never to return. Every time, she said her farewells, gave in to the facts, then turned around, went back inside, and threw herself into cleaning.

As happened when I disappeared, not through extinction but the collapse of one of the families of his species. For years after this, Turtle devoted herself to maintaining her vault and waxing the floors of her studio apartment. She went out for a bit of fresh air in the morning, dusted numerous surfaces, cleaned baseboards, inspected doors.

As for maintaining the roof, this she could only do from the inside; all outside cleaning she left to the rain. So whenever the sky opened up, she felt grateful: she'd never seen her own roof, but imagined it to be a gleaming, golden dome.

Every night she closed her shutters and fell asleep to the smell of cleaners. Rendering her own nothingness eternal, polishing it, fighting the malady of introspection with housework, was a recipe that saved her day after day, and permitted her to take another step for her species.

But now, for the past few days, Turtle hasn't been alone. While she was bustling about with house chores, while she was straightening up inside rather than sitting at her front door and making sure nothing was going on outside, there was construction happening all around.

And so she looked out one morning to find another home of her same species on the right, blocking her view. On the left, two other turtles, slightly smaller, but her exact model: carapace roof, perfectly geometrical, radial pattern on the shell.

The same fine architects, and evidently, the same Triassic Period.

And so, one day, Turtle became a row house. Even reptiles have petit bourgeois dreams. Her reaction is unclear, if she was a good neighbor or felt solidarity with her species, if there was gossiping on stoops, or just closed doors.

Hard to say where these three came from, if they were captured, in retreat. But along with them, one morning, a baby's feet appeared, and some high notes, and a tiny laugh.

A few moments of silence, then they all emerged from their shells, heads peeping out, unable to resist the call of infancy.

73

Home Inside the Fence, 2011

The overall view: the remnants of a lunch or dinner, shattered order, the disintegration of what was once whole: bread-crumbs, wine dregs in glasses, a nearly empty water pitcher, tangerine peels lying on plates, and a general feeling of surrender and confusion. A detail: the chairs and the napkins—two napkins on the table, one refolded or possibly unused, the other spread out, stained but not crumpled—two others on chair seats, one on the floor, between a chair and the front door, which opens to the stairway.

The chairs are arranged much like the napkins. Two are neatly set back at the table, two sit at a diagonal from the table, some distance away, allowing for a quick exit from the meal. One chair looks like it was never used at all: it goes with the unused napkin and is closest to the kitchen—Mother's chair. The others, not to dwell on whose was whose, are the chairs of Father, Wife, Little Girl, and I. The napkin near the door is I's, but in and of itself, it doesn't suggest drama. More of a habit, really, or plain distraction: he always gets up at the end of a meal and forgets that he was just sitting at a dinner table. In this case, though, the meal did indeed go badly: with their knees, Wife and Little Girl pushed their chairs back under the table in the living room and left their napkins on their chairs and followed after I who was already at the door, leaving, while they said goodbye to Mother and Father.

The scene—the table in the living room, leaf added for the occasion—only includes the sound of three car doors shutting, then the engine starting, and the roaring of the Panda's bad muffler fading in the distance. The background is the usual background to the Home Inside the Fence, the other six gray cement cubes, the provincial boredom of the surrounding neighborhood, dulled even more by Sunday.

Inside the Home, the sound of water running in the sink, which, along with the dish soap and Mother's hands, attempts to wash the memory from the dishes and return everything back to how it was before the meal, by putting it all away in the sideboard. After this comes the tablecloth and the washing machine, and the leaf swallowed up inside the table, the ceramic amphora returned to the center.

Father is sitting out on the balcony, a veteran of compromised meals, this time without shouting or theatrics. Even his brief threat, addressed to Wife—referring to her tumor, wishing her a speedy recurrence in a turn of phrase that wasn't even vague, compensation for I's removal from the family tree—spilled out, unnoticed, only truly shocking Little Girl.

What's left now in this silence is running water in the sink, and the scoffing of birds in the lone tree inside the fence, their ceaseless, scoreless singing. No trace of the goodbye at the door, the proxemics of it not unusual, just Mother's comment to her son that slipped away—a love plea, blackmail of the heart—but adding a tawdry touch to the meal: "It's either us or them, last night on the books."

And then, just that, the table pushed back together, and the car thirty kilometers north of there, plains all around, I at the wheel, Wife beside him, not speaking, her hand on his right leg, sometimes caressing his thigh. And Little Girl, in the back, staring at the nape of his neck, perhaps thinking that I looks like his parents or about their home or more likely, about something else, her eyes closed, head against the window. And Wife, finally, turning on the radio, trying to tune to something that will help them defend against their own boredom and independence, while they watch the stubborn, poignant expanse of countryside go by.

74

Home of Dispersal, 2019

THE LOCATION, ORAL VERSION, IS "past the highway exit on the right." But as far as GPS is concerned, it doesn't exist, or rather, it's a trick: the female voice sends you someplace else. A spot where there's nothing, just a white sign by a country road: AD SPACE FOR SALE 014-153-9440.

And while customers and owners have complained and pointed this out, little has changed in terms of placing this spot on the map: basically the response has been, We'll tell the satellite to be more careful.

From an architectural point of view, the Home of Dispersal is a prefab metal building. Which you actually reach by taking the interchange and spiraling down, proceeding on for six more kilometers. After the toll, the bar rises on a scene of similar warehouses, automatic gates, bobtail trucks, vans with open doors, forklifts in motion.

This is productive desolation, and kept outside the city walls. The heart of the planet, what makes it rotate on its profit axis, but that's also repressed. Not to be seen in a world of disappearance, the miracle of goods found on the doorstep. This is where that miracle occurs, where packaging is carried out; millions of tons of products, plastic and cardboard, the immense, unimaginable skeleton of postmodern lightness.

In this scenario, the Home of Dispersal is only a hangar, a parallelepiped among many others.

Outside the Home, an accumulation of items, hard to see the criteria here. A brief listing: sinks turned over on the ground (of fine gravel, a distant memory of former asphalt), a bunch of bidets and toilets. Plus: a pair of metal bed frames, winter tires, boots and shoes, some missing a mate, a bicycle without a seat, a shopping cart, a half-deflated donut floatie with a withered ducky inside. The rest is a pile of seemingly random items, fallen out of use.

This could be mistaken for a garbage dump, if the objects and furnishings weren't in fairly good shape. There's next to no rust: a little on a Fiat Punto door leaning against the wall, a sprinkling on the washing machine drum with the indoor clothesline coiled up inside. What this means, then, is that everything here is ready to be sold, put back in circulation.

To complete the general picture, just step inside—there's a massive sliding door, hard to open on your own. Here, in this space of about a thousand square meters, with glacial neon lighting running across the ceiling, you'll find the remnants of hundreds of previous lives, disassembled, rearranged inside this warehouse, and put up for sale at a humiliating price, considering their value. Each object bears a tag with a figure written in felt-tip pen, then lowered, then scratched out, then rewritten, a thousand times over, with the sole purpose of being sold and liquidated.

There are no aesthetic criteria here, no complete sets of anything. This is household furniture that's been cleared away and paired indifferently with other items: cheap veneer set alongside fine mahogany, the cupboard removed from its kitchen, now perched on top of an Empire-style highboy.

While chaotic, there is a division into household zones. Home appliances are located in the right back corner of the building. Among the refrigerators are former built-ins, plastic and metal, bodiless souls; others stand with their doors yawning open, showing yellowed interiors, sliding egg holders. Some are tall and riddled with stickers (like the furniture taken from the rooms of former teenagers, now set sideways, out of sorts, not far from the freezers); others are waist-high, remnants of temporary lives, few home-cooked meals.

At the center of the hangar, long tables are lined up in a row and stacked with dishes. Dinnerware sets, most of them incomplete: six missing one piece only, often a dinner plate. Early twentieth-century fine Majolica, floral pattern—fairly tasteful—set beside heavy bowls, nostalgic children of the Boom, triumphantly white, thin yellow or blue line running around the edge—indicative of large numbers, little small talk, and widespread well-being.

The common denominator: many of these dishes are chipped; so are the glasses, and they're in fewer complete sets; as are the mugs and sets of espresso cups, with some of these sitting on old—sometimes very old—tarnished silver trays.

Scattered about are piles of silverware, Scotch-taped bundles, a couple of euros for twenty-four knives, forks, soup spoons, and teaspoons that lived for decades in a dining room, then wound up here, along with everything else, a few saltshakers with slightly clogged holes, and corkscrews, pale green plastic egg cups, skimmers, sets of ashtrays from failed restaurants.

All of it in this vast space, this building so close to the highway bridge, the mass grave of the Millennium, where the West goes shopping. Failure sold at a bargain-basement price, dwellings drained through death and bankruptcy, homes auctioned off—sometimes out of disinterest, boredom with a style, with ownership; or an inheritance liquidated by the beneficiaries, horrified at the progenitors' tastes, more interested in brick and mortar than dishes. But also: the perfect market for furnishing new homes on very little, fitting out entire apartments, combining the improbable, randomly juxtaposing anachronisms. A place where the present replenishes itself for its collages, its mosaics of consigned, dusty, twentieth-century shards.

Dispersed in all of this is I's furniture, everything he's dragged around for decades, from apartment to apartment, everything that had been joined, finally, to the aesthetic world of Wife and Little Girl.

It would be useless, uselessly tedious, to track down each separate piece, those things which, put together, create a sense of home. Not to mention the possibility that some or all of it has been sold. What is certain: it's an entire world that I has gotten rid of, dismantled and dispersed in the same space as other losers' finished worlds.

The wardrobes are with the wardrobes—all those poor things posing in their own separate style—the chairs with the chairs, the dishes piled on top of the tables. Each object, each piece of furniture with its misshaped price tag/ID number slapped on. Everything put together for potential buyers to consider, wardrobe doors opened and slammed shut, forks inspected, tines tested with fingertips, then dropped back on the table, in a scene of general chaos.

I has never set foot in here, hasn't provided his bank information to the business so he can receive the low percentage of the small amount he's to get in the future for the last twenty years. The truth is, he doesn't even know the address; he knows it's under the highway, and that's enough for him to imagine the vertical drop of everything he owned: twenty years of wandering from Home to Home with furniture bought in bulk with a cashier's check, mistreated in hurried moves, crammed onto freight elevators, or hauled by hired arms, set down sometimes in the light, other times humiliated in the space of a temporary room, dismantled, put back together, every time, pushed up against a wall. And now, a sense of peace, in this final fall from the bridge, where you never look because you're driving, and I's not looking either, as he passes overhead and turns right, ignoring the ashes of his past dispersed by the handful over the urbanized landscape.

75

Friendship Home, 2020

WHEN TAKEN AS A WHOLE, it's endless, a railway junction, the last railway junction in Rome or else the first arriving from the North. The detail, however—so the actual Home—is a platform. To be precise: a few meters behind the yellow line, a step or two from the track. The track is mainly number 6, though with frequent last-minute changes announced, too, if a train is late or something's happened along the route. The Friendship Home announces its own appearance on a lit board: it stands out, fluorescent, in the middle of the other destinations in a column. It tells you where and for how long you'll be able to see it, like a comet.

And I looks for it here, after getting off the train he took through Rome—the gasometri always on the right, the aching yellows and oranges of Testaccio's low-rise buildings—which then continued on its way, over the trestles, headed toward Sabina. I raises his chin in the atrium in Tiburtina Station, makes his way through the crowd, and catches the Home on the scrolling list, while some flashing cities suddenly disappear in a landslide of destinations. Sometimes the Home's not there yet, and then it's just a matter of paying attention:

I stares at the board as he would the sky, and so do all the other people there. Then he suddenly steps back from the group.

The Friendship Home appears around 8:05, if the flow of trains is uninterrupted from Milan to the South. The Home's expanse coincides with the space I occupies as he waits for his high-speed train headed north, his daypack at his feet, with his laptop inside, and a change of clothes, if he decides he'll stay overnight. The Home becomes the Home for real when I's body reaches the body of another who's arrived out of breath after running through the underpass from track 1. Someone who's come from the countryside and stops in Rome; at night, he'll do it all in reverse. The embrace of these two men with their slightly graying beards is the front door, its hinges oiled by this customary act.

The amount of time the Home appears varies, but it's rarely for more than eleven minutes and is always a countdown. Inside the Home, there's always happy, excited conversation. Everything crammed in that hasn't been said: all of it in fragments, a minor bit of news alongside a disaster, a book just read, a worry of some kind, summer plans. They shake the dice cup of their bodies, and what they roll is what they'll know about each other the following day. Meanwhile I keeps his eye on the end of the track, that is, toward Rome, and if he sees the nose of his train, he hoists his backpack onto his shoulders while the conversation continues.

At 8:05 the Friendship Home appears; at 8:14 it usually fades away. What remains, invisible, is that meter and a half of good mood on the track, which over the course of a half hour will be trampled on by numerous other shoes. The Home will reappear after ten days, a month, will light up on the board, then disappear again.

76

Home of the Tumor, 2009

THE FEELING I GETS HERE is of deception, with the building's silhouette against the clear sky, out in the countryside—the mountains, behind, cornering the view. It's in the solid silence of the structure, the emptiness it carves from the landscape. In the solid nature of the building, while a world war rages inside.

This deception is only amplified when the doors slide open, activated by the photocell sensor. When I steps inside, an ice film forms over him, shaping how he appears beside Wife, who just enters with a hello and gets two greetings in return, and two smiles.

Wife steps inside like a veteran of death; I's been privileged, has walked through life brusquely, so his good health makes him feel a bit ashamed, and somehow insignificant.

The elevator first hesitates, then rises with flawless determination: a number flashes, indicating the floor, and on the fourth, the door opens with mechanical precision. Then, a long hallway, and a bald lady rolling down it in a wheelchair, a nurse pushing her.

Wife knows how to greet others here and does it naturally; I's natural courtesy turns to rhetoric. He takes Wife's hand, joins her body as a precaution. The wheelchair disappears onto the elevator. Wife touches I softly. The doctor's door opens, shuts with them both inside.

Leaving the building is what's most important: the countryside bursting open all around. The elevator stays open on the main floor; Wife and I's goodbye lingers in the lobby.

This time it's I who takes Wife out, to the side of life.

After reviewing her charts, running his fingers over her clean, now-faded scar line, the doctor said the tumor was cured. As of now, he said simply, no show of emotion, she had the same probability of dying as anybody else.

We'll see each other in five years, he said as he was leaving.

Not much to say about the trip home, I driving, like always. Wife has taken off her shoes, tucked her feet under her on the seat, and is back to the crossword puzzle she was working on before they got to the Home of the Tumor. Sometimes she tells him a clue and I thinks of a word; if it's right she says, "Good"; otherwise she just says, "No."

The rest of the talk is banal, even in memory. The miracle remembered that day, instead, is that they found parking right below their building.

77

Home of Notes, 2021

THE HOME OF NOTES IS a home of self-propelling words; I's production has moved there. He doesn't go in every morning; he opens the door when he feels like it. Technically, it's a notebook. With eighty-one pages, and an equal number of apartments.

The notes are sentences in rough shape, barely subsisting. Disjointed, bruised; they'd never be permitted to live inside a book.

A single entrance, a plain door. Black cardboard.

The eighty-one dwellings are all in a row—a quirk of the architect. Which means that to reach one down the line, you have to pass through all those before it. Those who arrive first, take their place first; here, you proceed through occupation.

In that the spaces are assigned by order of arrival, it's only natural that a dwelling winds up hosting notes without that much in common. But cohabitation has never really been an issue. At times, someone draws a line down the middle of a room, but for the most part, everyone lives in harmony.

—

There isn't just one Home of Notes.

Whenever all the spots are taken, I starts another notebook, and so the allocation, for those new sentences, of other housing in other buildings.

Same front door, same row, same routine.

In certain periods, the homes fill with notes within the week; others remain half-empty even for a month.

When they start to arrive, however, it's always a flow of words that doesn't seem to stop. You never know what might trigger that rushing swarm of notes. Peace or war, happiness or pain.

Sometimes I comes to check on them, inspecting the buildings, one after the other. He checks on their condition, the wear and tear on the fixtures, does some maintenance work.

He goes into the apartments to see what the phrases inside have to say to him. It's the most unpredictable part of the inspection. They all rush to talk at once—they want to be heard.

The reason the notes all gather around I: they know he holds the power. It's by his choice or whim that one of them will be taken, destined for someplace else.

A kind of social climbing. The hoped-for miracle of every note: to become a sentence. When this happens, the note packs up its trunks, strolls through the building, then heads down the road that no one's ever returned from, that carries you to a new life on a printed page.

78

Home of Escaped Memories

THINK ABOUT I ON AN early morning in November, at dawn, standing before the apparatus of his escaped memories. Always the same image: a Plexiglas box with a mechanical arm and crab claw that tries to grab hold of what's lying at the box's sandy bottom. Always the same sequence: the longing for a memory and then frustration, trying to claw that memory back. And so: a coin slipped into the slot, mechanical arm in action, crab claw lowering, pincers open. Then groping in the sand, claw rising again, empty, yet another in an endless line of failed attempts.

Seen through the Plexiglas, I, concentrating, then enraged, pounding the Plexiglas with his fist. Once more, the coin, once more, the disappointment.

But on this early morning in November, I starts to kick the apparatus. The crab claw keeps grabbing at memories but not pulling them from the sand. They're apparitions, holding on for an instant, then letting go, falling, disappearing into sand. And now I stops, furious, throws himself against the Plexiglas, kicking and punching. One final push, the apparatus falls over, and he leaves.

—

And so the Home of Memories opens its door, but too late: I could step inside, but he's far away now, his back to the Home: a disappearing dot.

The Plexiglas has cracked in the fall; the crack is widening. All the sand is pouring out, an avalanche of dust and memories spreading over the ground. She might be freed, but perhaps she's only scattered outside the door, homeless. The mechanical crab claw lies half-open, in a frozen, broken spasm.

What was once the Home of memories escaped from I's memory is now only a desecrated cemetery, and I won't return to see what's at the bottom of this home, and he won't stand it back upright. He'll accept that these memories are lost, that they never happened; he'll say the pronoun "I" and accept that fiction is the consequence of choice.

I won't see this landscape strewn with wreckage and sand, this landfill of memories that haven't found their place in any of the Homes he's lived in; they're relics at the bottom of the sea while up above, on the surface, other ships slide by.

And so I won't see the police cars, sirens flashing, racing toward Prisoner's dead body found in the trunk of a parked car; won't see the helicopters slicing the sky over Rome, searching for the fugitives; won't see the frightened people at their windows; won't see Relatives talking about Poet's death and crossing themselves; won't see Grandma hiding the wine bottle under the sink; won't see her stagger, and insult Mother; won't hear Grandma's voice on the telephone asking him for help; won't see himself hang up, then go back to what he's doing; won't see Wife spread her arms wide, taking him in, rescuing him; won't see himself promise her that they'll always be together; won't see himself happy, thanking her before going to sleep, for giving him a Home, or buying her flowers on Sunday mornings; won't hear her crying while he pretends to sleep; won't see their embrace, the incongruous yet complete tenderness of it, the moment they're divorced; won't see himself promise Little Girl he'll be her father even if they share no genes; won't see Father carrying him on his shoulders, when I is little, and letting him slip into the sea for the first time, holding him as he floats in the water; won't see Sister help him onto a bike, won't hear her adult voice, over the phone, saying, "You're a coward"; won't see Mother turn around when Father slams I against the kitchen wall, screaming, "I'll kill you"; won't see her brush a fly from his head when he's a teenager, asleep on the couch, or see her waiting for him outside his kindergarten with a heavy sweater; won't see himself, I, take Father's hand as they go down the stairs; won't see Mother's face that last time in the Home Inside the Fence, and her asking him, "Will you be back?" and his own mouth saying, "Sure," not knowing yet that this would never happen.

He won't see any of this because he's already far away; even the dot has dissolved on this early morning in November. The wind is up; it might bring snow. The snow will spread a white blanket over this landscape of shipwrecked memories. The snow is cold but will hold in the heat, and protect the ground.

Acknowledgments

This is the first book I'm publishing as a permanent resident in the U.S. And that stirs up a lot of feelings for me, as well as the usual question of belonging. Which, as we all know, is an impossible question to answer. Which makes it a literary question.

But publishing this book as a "green card guy" also stirs up a lot of gratitude for me, for the people and institutions that are making room for me and my work in this new life I'm now living on the west side of the Atlantic. So: thanks to Rice University, in particular to the Dean of Humanities, Kathleen Canning, and to all my colleagues in the English Department and in the Creative Writing Program: without your support and nourishment I couldn't be the writer I am in this part of my life and this part of the globe. I'm deeply grateful to the energizing crew at Deep Vellum; to Rich Levy and Krupa Parikh at Inprint; to Basket Books and Brazos Bookstore; to Jill Schoolman and the whole team of Archipelago Books; to Barbara Epler at New Directions, Edwin Frank at NYRB, and Daniel Gumbiner at *The Believer*. To the American Academy in Rome, in particular to Aliza Wong. To Comites Houston, ISNNAF and Mauro Lorenzini at the Consolato Generale d'Italia a Houston. To Beatrice Monti della Corte and the Santa Maddalena Foundation in Tuscany, Italy. To Costica Bradatan, Geoffrey Brock, Michael Cunningham, Nick Flynn, Richard Ford, Andrew Sean Greer, Mark Haber, Rodrigo Hasbún, Jhumpa Lahiri, Katie Kitamura, Alberto Manguel, Maaza Mengiste, Roberto Tejada, Anderson Tepper, Colm Toíbín, Minna

Zallman Proctor, John Sparagna, and Edmund White. And to Liz Harris, who dances with every phrase I write in Italian as she spins it into musical English. Finally, to my little bilingual family that makes my life more meaningful, no matter which side of the ocean we're on.

I feel I belong to this gratitude. It's a warm place to be, a wonderful embassy. Just like literature, the only institution I know where no passport's required. Gratitude and literature don't need a house to exist.

Andrea Bajani
Houston, Texas, March 2025

Andrea Bajani was born in Rome in 1975. He is the author of many award-winning novels, including, in English translation, *If You Kept a Record of Sins* (Archipelago, 2021, translated by Elizabeth Harris) and *Every Promise* (MacLehose Press, 2013, translated by Alistair McEwan). He is currently a writer in residence at Rice University in Houston, Texas.

Elizabeth Harris's recent translations from Italian include works by Antonio Tabucchi, Francesco Pacifico, Claudia Durastanti, and Andrea Bajani, with Archipelago Books, FSG, Riverhead Books, and Fitzcarraldo Editions. She has received numerous grants and awards for translation, including an NEA Translation Fellowship and the National Translation Award.

9 781646 053810